ZEKE PROPER
AND THE SACRIFICE AT ALDER COVE

By Brad Cameron

First published by Dog Ear Publishing
4010 W. 86th Street, Ste H
Indianapolis, IN 46268
www.dogearpublishing.net

ISBN: 978-160844-580-6

This book is printed on acid-free paper.

Printed in the United States of America

PROLOGUE

Rumors

In Alder Cove there are some who say that wandering by yourself at night, especially in the surrounding hills that border the town, is suicide: there are things out there that will eat you. They say the river is haunted and that swimming there, in that deep, dark, cold water is treacherous. The current is strong, but worse, something lives there, and she, yes, she, will grab you and pull you under, swallowing you in one, painful gulp.

It has also been said that Alder Cove has an invisible wall surrounding it; that this wall is permeable only from the outside. You can go in easily enough, but getting out is another story.

But these are just rumors.

There are some who will tell you that the founding fathers of the town brought about a curse that is still present today, and that the first inhabitants were giants who were guided over the sea by the hand of a forgotten god. They say that Odin, the gentle leader of souls, reached down from the heavens and touched the white stones with his finger, illuminating them from the inside, their iridescences lighting the darkness of their voyage and chasing away the demons and devils that would try to hinder their journey. They say that the travelers were comforted by the etchings on the stone's surfaces, their exteriors embedded with strange writings: the runes of a lost language.

But again, these are just rumors. Who, really, can say which is true and which is not?

CHAPTER 1

From the Depths

Mayor David Vernon sat comfortably in his overstuffed leather chair, his posture relaxed, his head lolling on the head rest. With the tips of his feet, he swiveled round and round like a small child at the counter in a malt shop. Finally, after becoming light headed from the spinning, he stopped his rotation and faced the large picture window that took up one entire wall of his office in Town Hall. From his position, he was presented with an expansive view of Alder Cove. The vista before him offered him a majestic glimpse of the bay that edged the small town. Fishing vessels could be seen arriving from the open water along with a gentle but sweet smelling sea breeze that seemed to accompany their appearance. White fluffy clouds with a brilliant blue background stood out bright and clear. And seagulls circled lazily in the warm spring sky, crying out their farewell anthem to the close of another day.

The Mayor took great delight in his surroundings: rich, lavish and ornate, all of the comforts his mind could conceive. And yet, today, he remained contemplative and concerned. Something wasn't right, and he couldn't quite place his finger on just what that something was.

In his reverie, he recalled the way the streets of Alder Cove were once filled with people walking the sidewalks, greeting each other as they passed. But the shops and stores, now empty of tourists that usually combed the streets of Alder Cove during the summer months, were extremely sparse. He recalled that it was only last summer when families would play in the park, swim in the public pool, gather for picnics along the beach and fill the local baseball diamond grandstands to watch the local teams play. Now, he thought sadly, the people, the pools, the streets and the beaches remained empty and somehow hollow, as did most of the other parts of Alder Cove.

"My town is dying" he said to no one in particular, "and I fear that I may know the reason why." He sighed heavily taking a gentle puff on his expensive cigar, tapping the ashes into a marble tray that sat on the corner of his costly desk. "Once again, I'm afraid, something drastic must be done before it disappears completely; before this place rots back into the earth from whence it came."

Mayor Vernon heaved himself out of his chair, his big belly brushing the front of the desk, and waddled heavily over to the small reception office where his secretary, Miss Marjorie Anders, sat typing. He looked at her sadly, remembering when she too used to have a happier countenance and a welcoming smile. But that was many years ago. *Too many sacrifices,* the mayor thought. *It is too much to ask of one woman. But we must do what we must do.*

The mayor inched himself further into the room. "Ahem" he croaked, making a kind of low pitched nasally sound to accompany the clearing of his throat.

Miss Anders looked up from her typing. She appeared slightly annoyed at the interruption and, looking over her reading glasses, looked menacing. "Yes, Mayor Vernon, how may I help you?"

The Mayor moved apprehensively to Miss Anders' desk. He suddenly admitted to himself that as of late he had become a bit fearful of Miss Anders. The bitterness that was evident on her face as she looked at him made him wonder whether the wealth and prosperity of a small town was worth it. However, the mayor reminded himself that it was. "May I bother you with a question, Miss Anders?" wincing slightly with the thought that Miss Anders would suddenly begin yelling at him for the unnecessary interruption.

"I *suppose* I could stop my *important* work for your...question," she said sarcastically.

The mayor ignored her sarcasm and went on. "We...you and I, I mean, have always been friends, Miss Anders," and this wasn't a question as much as a statement of fact. Mayor Vernon and Miss Anders had always been close. They practically grew up together. As children, the Mayor and Miss Anders lived next door to each other. And though the Mayor was two years older than Miss Anders they had become well associated through Marjorie's brother, John. David and John were best friends, or had been, until that night thirty years ago near the river that lay to the south of the town. No one really spoke of that night anymore, and when anyone started to bring up the subject, the topic was quickly shifted to something more pleasant. Nevertheless, both David and Marjorie remained friends, though the bitterness and regret had taken its toll.

Marjorie's expression seemed to soften a little at the Mayor's statement. "Yes, David, you and I have been friends for quite some time. Is that the question you wanted to ask?"

"Well, no..." he stuttered. "What I mean is, have you noticed something different lately? -about the town I mean?"

Marjorie shifted in her seat uncomfortably. She removed her glasses and began cleaning them on the front of her blouse. "Well, now that you mention it, yes, I have noticed things being a bit...unsettled as of late."

"Unsettled...yes, well not quite the way I'd put it." The mayor began scratching his chin. He leaned in a bit closer to Miss Anders and in a barely audible whisper said, "Do you remember that night, Marjorie? Thirty years ago? John and the river?"

Marjorie gasped. She brought her hand to her throat as if to protect herself from something ugly and menacing. She looked about the room as if somebody might have heard. "No, I mean, yes, but..." Then in a sharp whisper of her own said, "We aren't supposed to talk about that!"

"Yes, I know, but do you remember just before we discovered," and he cupped his hands around his mouth and drew in even closer to Miss Anders' ear and whispered, "the *wonderful* secret? The things that *made* us what we *are* today?"

Miss Anders drew back from the Mayor quickly. She brought her hand up to her mouth, her lips formed in a horror stricken O; her eyes reflecting sudden fear and understanding. "You're not suggesting...?" she stammered.

"Well, I'm only guessing, really. I mean, things do seem very similar, don't they?" Moreover, they *were* very similar. In fact, the hair on the back of Mayor Vernon's neck began to stand on end as he considered the frightening yet refining possibility.

"If it is what you're suggesting, David, then...we may have to..."

"Indeed," interrupted the Mayor.

"I can't...I can't go through that again!" She was still whispering, but her voice was frantic; her breath coming out in short bursts of air.

The Mayor grabbed hold of both of her shoulders. He shook her gently, trying to calm her sudden panic. "Marjorie...Marjorie, listen to me!" he said, forcing her to look into his eyes. "We know what must be done. You know how it works. There is nothing we can do about it. Now, calm yourself and try to focus on the future," he said, raising his pudgy purple lips into a smile. "The bright, prosperous future of Alder Cove."

However, what Marjorie Anders saw was not a smile. *No*, she thought, *not a smile, a sneer*. The Mayor's beady eyes seemed to project a disturbing vision of anticipation and pleasure.

David Vernon shuffled himself back into his ornate office and closed the door. As he eased himself down into his chair, the aroma of leather exhaled into the air. With shaking hands, he reached toward his desk and opened one of the lower drawers. Inside were a few files and folders that acted only as decoys for the real purpose of the drawer. The Mayor removed the contents and released a small bronze latch that concealed a hidden false bottom. He turned the latch gently to the left and then slid it back toward the front of the drawer. A small click was heard as the bottom lifted, exposing a highly polished wooden box. On the front of the box was an ancient looking key hole. David Vernon reached inside the front of his shirt and brought out a silver skeleton key that hung on a string dangling loosely around his neck. *The key to the city*, David thought. *How ironic*. And he chuckled to himself, knowing that as far as inside jokes go, this one was one of those you-had-to-be-there kind. He placed the key into the lock and turned. Again, a subtle click was heard. He lifted the lid, staring inside, his eyes widening with anticipation as a glimmer of reflected light shone on the polished surface of 24 black stones. "Time to make a call," he said out loud to no one in particular.

* * * * *

The small fishing vessel rose and fell gently on the waves. Its captain, a short, portly, wizened old man of the deep, sat upright, hands on the wheel, guiding the boat expertly toward home. His small crew of men were at the rear of the craft tending to the nets that had just been pulled from the ocean, empty - again.

The captain bowed his head and gritted his teeth in frustration. Two weeks now and none of the fishing boats had pulled anything from the sea. It's like, *thought the old man,* like a time many years ago. *He shuddered at the thought. Suddenly, a shadow pervaded the deck of the boat. Yet this shadow, oddly enough, was not the result of an object that blocked the light of the fading sun, but from a presence that seemed to lurk beneath the bow of the vessel; a presence that darkened the boat, not with a physical shade, but with one that darkened the minds of those that stood upon its deck.*

The sailors, abandoning the repair and stowage of the nets, ran to the sides of the boat and leaned over, looking into the depths, fear mingled with curiosity as they tried to determine the cause of the darkness. Suddenly, a massive form appeared. The already darkened sea became black against its hulk. It drifted underneath the boat, and the sailors ran to the opposite side of the vessel to observe its advance. It moved steadily, gliding its way toward land in the direction of the small town that lay in the distance.

The sailors continued to watch as the immense form drifted farther away from the boat, and though they felt no fear of being attacked by the...whatever it was, they felt - what? Hopelessness? Despair? Or perhaps - foreboding.

CHAPTER 2

A Proper Reunion

The ride was anything but smooth as the U-Haul chugged its way along the coastal highway north, away from Halifax toward Alder Cove. In the cab of the truck, Zeke Proper stared out the window as the rocky landscape rushed by. He noted, with pleasure, the picturesque view of the ocean crashing against rugged shorelines, the gentle flight of seabirds winging their way just inches above the surface of the turbulent water, and the fabulous blue sky that seemed to accentuate the entire scene making it worthy of a valued post card. The view made Zeke feel content, though the challenging events of the last week still tugged at his memory. Leaving his home in Halifax was difficult. He grew up there. It was all he knew. All of his friends were there and he would miss them tremendously, especially Cindy. But his mom and dad had both promised him that he could call her once a week. And before the summer was over, he was assured that another trip back to Halifax for a visit could be arranged.

The move to Alder Cove was unexpected and quick; the family barely had time to pack. Zeke's father had put their home up for sale as soon as he was offered the position as Alder Cove's new city planner, and it had sold quickly, too quickly for Zeke's comfort and certainly too quickly for his mother's. She, more than any of the other family members, argued the most against leaving. To Vivian Proper a move two hours north of their established home was excessive, especially with only one week's notice. She just couldn't understand why Percy Proper, Zeke's father, found it so necessary to rush the move to Alder Cove. As a result, life around the Proper home had been tense. Zeke's parents were constantly fighting, and Zeke often felt like he was walking on eggshells around his parents, always aware that one wrong word might start a new argument.

As the moving van rounded a tight corner bringing them even closer to their new home, Percy Proper began talking about his own youth growing up in Alder Cove. Zeke was aware that his father was trying to instill in him a sense of enthusiasm for the move, though to Zeke it would take more than just a few stories to get him excited about abandoning his friends in Halifax.

They rounded another corner and suddenly came in view of some distant buildings. Percy Proper seemed to sit a little taller in his seat, though Zeke noted that his posture appeared stiff and uncomfortable. They soon came in sight of an ancient looking wooden bridge spanning a narrow river. As they crossed over, Percy abruptly stopped talking. His mood became dark, as if a black storm cloud had drifted into the cab of the truck. Zeke suddenly felt that "eggshell" feeling again as he too remained quiet, fearing some outburst from his father if he happened to say the wrong thing. In quiet they continued along into the center of Alder Cove, passing a marina filled with idle fishing boats and a deserted, somewhat dilapidated, downtown sector. The truck came to a sudden stop as they approached the first of two traffic lights in the town. No other traffic was in observed and Zeke felt it odd that they should be waiting at a red light when there were no other cars.

"Dad," Zeke said as he shifted uncomfortably on the hot, sticky, vinyl seats of the moving van. The traffic light had changed to green and his father, instead of continuing forward, stared straight ahead with a glassy look in his eyes. He was evidently preoccupied with something other than driving their belongings to their new home.

Zeke noted that ever since they had come in sight of Alder Cove, five miles back on the old coast highway, his father's mood had drastically changed. One minute he was happily retelling old adventures about the good old days growing up in Alder Cove, the next minute Zeke's father shifted to a deep silence, one that entirely pervaded the cab of the truck. As the light continued to glare an frantic green, Zeke's father remained motionless, staring out the windshield of the van.

"Dad, it's green," Zeke repeated.

"Hm...what?" Mr. Proper suddenly came out of his deep reverie at the sound of his son's voice and the honking of a car's horn behind them.

"It's green, the light, it's green. You can go now." Zeke repeated urgently.

"Oh, green. So it is." Mr. Proper quickly shifted the heavy truck into gear with a roaring, grinding of the gears. The truck lurched forward and they proceeded down the road. However, Mr. Proper remained silent as they made their way up Main Street.

"You okay?" Zeke asked, suddenly concerned that something might be very wrong. "You're not angry are you?"

"Angry? No. Why would I be angry?" Mr. Proper turned to his son, he smiled, but Zeke could tell something *was* wrong. His father was smiling with his lips, but his eyes showed something else. Zeke could have sworn it was fear.

* * * * *

After a short drive, the bulky U-Haul turned onto Pike Street and pulled up to their new home. Zeke, excited to have arrived after an exhausting two hours of driving, exited the moving van and ran to the front door.

Behind the van there pulled up a large paneled station wagon containing plants, boxes and the rest of the Proper family: Mrs. Vivian Proper, Devon, Zeke's younger brother, and Rufus, the family dog. The doors practically exploded open, as Devon and Rufus also exited the confines of the car. Mrs. Proper slowly and grudgingly swung herself out of the driver's seat. She stood looking at the new home with a grim, forlorn expression. She rested her hands on the small of her back, arching and stretching so as to work out the kinks she had developed from the long drive.

Zeke stood at the front door frantically, and vainly, trying to open it. He then realized that his mother had the keys. "Come on mom!" he shouted, "I want to see my new room!"

"Okay!" she playfully shouted back, "don't get your shorts in a knot!" Then, ignoring her son's anxious beckoning, turned to her husband who had just stepped out of the cab of the truck.

"Well, we're here," she said, her mood quickly changing to concern and apprehension. "Though I'm still not convinced this was the best choice. Moving our family at the last minute like this just doesn't make sense. Things were going so well in Halifax. I just don't understand why taking this job, here of all places, was so important."

"Don't start with me again!" he said sharply, though his voice was hushed to a severe whisper. "I have my reasons, I've told you that, so you'll just have to trust me. Working for the town of Alder Cove could be a great opportunity for this family, besides, I grew up here and I turned out okay."

Vivian's eye's narrowed. "Right now that seems a little questionable. It isn't like you to be so angry. Are you sure everything is alright?" she asked.

"Yes, I'm fine, we're fine, everything is fine, so just drop it," Percy Proper exclaimed.

Vivian pushed on, despite her husband's outburst. "Percy," she said, gently placing her hands to the sides of his face and forcing him to look at her. "You seem...distant. There's something you're not telling me and I'm worried." She was looking at him now with a softened, almost motherly expression on her face.

He hesitated, taking in a deep breath. "I guess I'm just tired," he finally said, taking her hands from his face and holding them in his hands. "All of the long driving must have really pooped me out," but then, Vivian noticed Percy Proper's eyes glancing out over the not so distant hills that loomed over the small town of Alder Cove; a bleak shadow seemed to darken his features.

* * * * *

The late summer darkness was beginning to settle over the town. Zeke looked around his room as the light began to fade. He was quite satisfied with the way the room was set up. He had been working all afternoon putting together his bed, sliding his dresser and desk in place, hanging up his clothes and putting his personal items in order. He moved quietly over to the closet where a full-length mirror hung on the inside of the door. He pulled open the door. From its rusted hinges there issued a loud squeak. Zeke looked at himself in the reflection. He noticed that his jeans and t-shirt were smudged with dirt from the day's work of moving. He noted, too, that his normally tight, curly red hair hung down slightly over his piercing blue eyes, making him look even more disheveled, though the freckles crossing over his nose still seemed to gleam with a radiance of youth and vitality. The running he had been doing while training for his middle school's cross country team had allowed him to have a lean, healthy appearance. His skin was slightly tanned from his many hours spent outside, and his eyes reflected a certain self-confidence that absorbed and hid any kind of arrogance.

He crossed the room to a window seat that looked out over the street in front of his house. From his vantage point, he could see his father bringing in the last of the family's possessions from the rented moving van. Mrs. Proper was down in the kitchen unpacking dishes wrapped in newspaper and placing them gently in the kitchen cupboards, while Devon ran around the house holding a small metal replica of a World War II fighter airplane. Zeke could hear Devon making a "fart" sound with his tongue, vibrating and slightly protruding it from his mouth, mimicking the sound of an airplane's engine. Zeke laughed silently to himself, he could imagine the spit that must be accumulating along the walls and floors as Devon passed, shooting down his imaginary enemies.

Zeke yawned and quickly removed his dirty t-shirt and jeans and tossed them onto the floor in the middle of the room. Then, thinking better of what he had just done, effortlessly scooped them up and placed them on, not in, (that would be too neat) the laundry hamper. The last thing he needed, he thought, was his mother yelling at him because his room was already messy. Zeke then pulled on his pajamas, for though it was summer, the evenings in Alder Cove could become quite chilly, especially with the sea breezes that blew in from the bay. He propped and fluffed his pillow, placing it high up on the headboard. He then reached down and picked up a small, polished, intricately carved wooden box, placing it gently on the bed while he situated himself comfortably on the propped up pillow.

After wiggling himself into a snug position, Zeke took hold of the box. With his finger, he traced the letters he had burned into the lid with his wood burning kit. The words were abrupt, but the message was simple : **PROPERTY OF ZEKE PROPER - DO NOT DISTURB.** He placed the box squarely on his lap.

As he began to lift the lid, there came a soft knock at the door. Zeke jumped at the noise and quickly replaced the lid. Moving to his knees with the box tightly held in his arms, he bent over the side of the bed and shoved it under, concealing its whereabouts. The door opened gently and quietly. Zeke's mother poked her head into the room. "Someone's here to see you," she said, a slight mischievous smile just barely crossing her lips.

"Somebody... at the door, to see *me*? Now. At this time of *night*?" Zeke said incredulously.

"Yes, now put on some clothes and come and meet her."

"Meet *her*?" he asked. "You're kidding, right?"

Zeke's question was not all that strange. The problem was that sometimes Zeke's mom *was* kidding. She had a way of being a little child-like at times, and playing a practical joke on either Zeke or Devon was not too uncommon. For Vivian Proper the glass was always half-full and a laugh was better than a frown anytime, though lately her disposition had changed. It seemed that his mother and father had been fighting a great deal more than usual. The cause of the fights were still unknown to Zeke, but the tension could be felt in the air.

"Come on, silly," she said, her eyes bright with anticipation, "it's your cousin."

"My cousin?" Zeke simply stared at his mother. He hoped that the shocked look on his face would somehow convey the millions of questions he had running through his mind. "I didn't know I had a cousin here!"

"Well, second cousin really. But still, she's your cousin. So come on down and meet her, and hurry up. It's not nice to keep a lady waiting." Then with a bit of a girlish giggle, Zeke's mom left the room leaving Zeke sitting on the edge of his bed, his eyes wide with confusion, staring at the now vacant door-way.

With a slight shake of his head, Zeke soon came out of his shock and quickly reclaimed the discarded jeans and t-shirt from off the top of the laundry hamper. He removed his paja-mas and put back on the dirty clothes. Then, moving to the closet door and checking his hair in the reflection of the full-length mirror, deemed himself presentable for visitors.

Exiting his room, Zeke took a moment to listen, hoping he might pick up some clues about this late evening visitor. Unfor-tunately, all Zeke could make out were the sounds of Rufus barking and some muffled voices coming from the entryway near the front door.
Zeke again smoothed down the sides of his hair and tried in vain to brush off some of the day's accumulated dirt from his shirt and jeans. He then slowly made his way down the stairs to greet his cousin.

There, standing near the bottom of the stairs was one of the most unusual sights Zeke had ever seen. "Zeke," his mother said, as he placed his foot on the last step, "this is your cousin, Taylre Marjorie Anders." Then, with a formal gesture of her hand, pointed toward Zeke. "Taylre, this is Zeke."

All eyes, it seemed, were on Zeke, including Devon's, who stood nearby with a goofy little grin on his face, the one that Zeke hated. For Devon, at least from Zeke's perspective, was made of mischief. He never knew when to stifle his laughter, and at times it came during the most inappropriate times. Most recently it occurred last Thanksgiving when Zeke's mom and dad decided to invite an older couple who lived Near their home in Halifax to join them for dinner. They felt sorry for them because they had no family of their own to share the fes-tive meal. The evening wore on and everything seemed to be going well until the old woman leaned over to pick up her dropped napkin. As she bent over, leaning just a little too far, she lost her balance and started to tip over on her seat. Percy Proper moved quickly, lunging from his own seat and grabbing hold of the falling woman. The woman, shocked by the sudden plunge toward the carpet, let out a stream of curses and profanity, seldom, if ever, heard in the Proper home. Everyone else seated around the table stared in confused astonishment, their mouths gaping open in startled surprise. All, but Devon. He alone gurgled out a gush of laughter that spilled out of his mouth like coins pouring from a broken vending machine. Tears spilled from his eyes as the laughter overtook him. Zeke was embarrassed and ashamed, though the old woman seemed to be completely unaware of what she had just done. Devon's life, it seemed, was dedicated to making Zeke's life miserable. At least that's what Zeke thought. However, Zeke managed to ignore Devon for the time being and focus his attention on Taylre.

Taylre stood with her back to the dining room. She was only fourteen years old, but already stood almost six feet tall and was, as most onlookers would say, skinny as a rail. Her back was straight, though slightly hunched at the shoulders. Her hair was tightly curled and bright red, blending with the spattering of freckles that flowed across her cheeks and nose. She wore glasses that covered a large portion of her face which seemed to magnify her eyes five or six times their normal size. In terms of clothing, Taylre pretty much always wore the same thing: short bib overalls with a red and white striped t-shirt underneath. But, it wasn't that she only had these two items of clothing, in fact far from it. Taylre had seven pairs of the same pieces of clothing. Each one labeled in her closet with a different day of the week. When Taylre spoke, which was quite often, her speech was slurred by the glistening set of braces that she wore on her teeth. Nevertheless, when she smiled, as she often did, the result was contagious. She seemed to be immune to the sodden, downcast, nightmarish feelings that seemed to be overtaking the rest of the town. It was this smile that made

Zeke believe that Taylre was a kindred spirit; that their friendship, though they had only just met, had been around for years and years.

"I am *so* happy to meet you. You just have no idea!" Taylre said enthusiastically, sending drops of spittle in several different directions as she spoke. She extended her hand toward Zeke who took it with the impression that she wanted to shake his hand. However, instead of shaking, Taylre grabbed hold of Zeke and pulled him in close, giving him a tight, you-are-now-my-best-friend hug. Zeke stood still, his arms at his side, feeling short and a bit awkward.

Taylre then turned to Devon. She bent down to look him in the face. "And you. You are so cute. I could just eat you up." Then she hugged Devon and he earnestly returned the hug, something Zeke found odd considering Devon rarely allowed even his own mother to touch him. Taylre continued by kissing Devon hard on both cheeks. Devon stepped back grinning his annoying grin and giggling at the same time.

"I have been anticipating this moment for hours now. Things around here just haven't been the same. But now that you're here...well, let me just say, we...are going to have...a blast!" Then she smiled, giggled, and smiled some more, holding her hands to the sides of her face, as if trying to hold in all of her emotion.

Zeke smiled too, in spite of the touch of awkwardness he felt. He had never been around a person like Taylre before; he was both surprised and delighted.

The four of them, Zeke, Devon, Taylre and Mrs. Proper, all stood for a few moments in a kind of awkward silence; no speaking, just staring, while Rufus looked up at Taylre wagging his tail. Finally, the silence was broken. "Well," Taylre said, "I just wanted to say hello. My grandma said I could come over for just a quick stopover. I know it's late…but I was so excited I just couldn't wait to see you."

"I'm very glad that you did, Taylre." Mrs. Proper said, giving Zeke a sideways glance that seemed to say, *why don't you say something?*

Zeke, noticing his mother's subtle hint said, "And I'm really glad you came by too, Taylre, really, I am. I'm not usually this quiet, but I suppose I'm just a bit shocked to find out I even *have* a cousin. No one's ever told me before." This time Zeke gave his mother a sideways glance that seemed to say, *thanks for not telling me.*

"Oh, that's okay," Taylre said reassuringly, "my grandma just told *me* today. So don't feel so bad." There was another short moment of silence, and then Taylre reached for the door.

"Well, I suppose I should be going now, my grandma will be waiting up for me. But I'll see you tomorrow, okay? And I'll show you around the town, at least…" she stammered, thinking of a way to say what she truly wanted to say, but then changing her mind said, "anyway, I'll see you tomorrow, bright and early, okay?" Which was not really a question that was left hanging for Zeke's approval, but more of a statement of: *ready or not, here I come.*

Taylre flung open the door and ran down the front steps. She made her way across the street and down a half block to her own house with amazing speed; her long legs carrying her smoothly and quickly across the lawns and asphalt. Before entering her home she turned and waved at both Zeke and Devon who stood on their own front porch, mesmerized; they had never seen anyone run that fast before, especially not a girl.

"Well, she seems nice," Mrs. Proper said, closing the door, locking up the deadbolt and leaving Zeke, Devon and Rufus to themselves.

Standing inside the entry way of their house, Zeke looked down to see Devon staring up at him - that stupid grin again - "What are you lookin' at?" Zeke said.

"Oh, I don't know. An ugly monkey-face." Devon then ran up the stairs, knowing that Zeke would be right behind him, hands tightened into a fist, ready to pop Devon in the arm - which was true, except that Devon, though he was two years younger than Zeke, could out run him, a fact that frustrated Zeke even more. Rufus ran up the stairs behind them barking, assuming that it was all fun and games. Devon reached his room just ahead of Zeke and slammed the door in his face; turning the lock on the door just before Zeke could turn the knob. Behind the door, Devon could be heard laughing. "Maybe next time monkey-boy."

Zeke drew in a deep breath, filling his cheeks with air and furrowing his brow. Then he exhaled slowly. He knew that he would get him back, it was only a matter of patience. In the meantime, he retreated to his own room. He had more organizing to do.

CHAPTER 3

Dreams

The golden light of morning began to seep into Zeke's room. A faint glow from the sunrise covered his face as he lay in his bed. A soft, down comforter was bunched up around his chest while his legs and feet remained exposed, and Zeke's mouth hung open in complete relaxation while a trickle of slobber dampened the pillowcase, a soft snoring emanating from his throat. Suddenly, a small pebble, entering from the open window, struck Zeke in the forehead. He stirred uneasily, grunted slightly, and squeezed his eyes tightly and rolled over, resuming his sleep. Then, another pebble entered striking Zeke on the back of the head, this time much harder. Zeke sat up quickly, his eyes flying open, scanning the room for the source of the unexpected pain - gently rubbing the now tender spot at the back of his head. His first thought was that Devon had wandered into his room and took a jab at him just for spite. But then he quickly realized - as another pebble flew across the room and hit the wall - that the pain on his forehead and the back of his head didn't come from Devon, but from the occasional toss of a rock that was being launched into his room from somewhere below his open window.

He stepped tenderly onto the cold wooden floor, glancing momentarily at his alarm clock on his dresser - 6:30 am - and moved quickly to the open window, sliding it up even more so that his head and upper body could fit through. Looking down first into the open street, Zeke saw nothing. Then his gaze wandered closer to the house onto the front lawn itself. There, standing in her striped red and white t-shirt and short overalls was Taylre, bright eyed, smiling, her hands cupped around her mouth whispering sharply, "Get dressed, get your brother, and come on down...we have a lot to do today...let's get going, sleepy head!"

Sleepy head? Zeke thought, then aloud said, "It's six-thirty in the morning for crying out loud!" Taylre shrugged her shoulders, smiled and waited.

Zeke pulled himself back into the room, running his hands through his hair, yawning and then stretching his back. He then shook his head in resignation, realizing that Taylre would not give up so easily - going back to bed just wasn't an option.

He dressed quickly, putting on a clean t-shirt but opting to keep the dirty jeans - *no sense piling up the laundry too high*, he thought. He stopped by the bathroom to splash some water on his face and take care of business, then proceeded to Devon's room, grabbing hold of the knob as he had done the night before. Visions of getting back at his brother for the name calling kept passing through his mind. However, when he entered the room, intent on jumping on Devon's bed, pulling away his pillow and then smacking him with it, the visions quickly fled; Devon was already up and dressed.

Devon, always an early riser, was seated at a small table near the window of his room, the faint light of morning easing its way through the shear drapes. On the table was a sheet of paper that Devon was intently drawing on, his mind completely focused on his work, so much so that he seemed to be completely unaware that Zeke was in the room.

Zeke noted, as he crept up to Devon, still intent on scaring him a little, that Devon's tongue protruded slightly from the corner of his mouth, revealing intense concentration on his part. He also noticed that Devon worked quickly, making broad strokes with the black colored pencil he was using. As he got closer, looking just slightly over Devon's shoulder, Zeke was able to make out a somewhat disturbing, almost nightmarish scene that Devon was depicting on the paper. As he moved closer, a small *creak* escaped from a loose floorboard. Devon turned in an instant and stopped drawing, a small gasp of surprise sounding from his throat.

Devon, realizing that Zeke was standing right over him, moved quickly to cover up the drawing he had just made. "Quit sneaking up on me!" he shouted, now shielding the entire paper with his arms and head.

"I wasn't," replied Zeke. "I just came in to wake you. Taylre's outside and wants us to come and hang out."

Still keeping the paper covered with his arms, Devon raised his head at the sound of Taylre's name. "Taylre's here...already?"

"Yeah, she's standing out front." Then, trying to make it seem like an after thought said, "so what are you drawing. Looks kinda' scary."

Devon looked at Zeke for a long time with a strange kind of evaluating stare. Almost as if to say: *can I trust you?* "It's nothing," he said, taking the paper and tucking it underneath a small, spiral-ringed notebook.

"Just let me take a look at it...what's the big deal?" Zeke said, edging himself around the side of the desk.

"The big deal is that I don't want you to see it...you'll just make fun of it."

Zeke had to think a moment about that last comment. Usually he would make fun of Devon's - well, anything, really. His writing, drawing, playing. *It's just what big brother's did*, Zeke thought. But now, looking at the serious expression that Devon had on his face made Zeke rethink his initial impulse that was in fact to tease Devon for whatever his drawing might be. "I won't," Zeke finally said. "I mean...I promise not to make fun of your drawing."

Devon considered this for a moment and seeing something in Zeke's eyes that seemed to convince him, decided to let him see it. He gently pulled the drawing from beneath the notebook and held it out for Zeke to inspect. Zeke, looking at the drawing closer now, gave a short intake of breath, almost as if a small cube of ice had been dropped down the back of his shirt. "What is this?" he said incredulously. "It looks like something out of a horror movie. But not one that I'd ever like to see."

"It was the dream I had last night...that...that thing was in my dream. It woke me up so I went into mom and dad's room to sleep with them because I was so scared." Reflected in Devon's eyes there still lingered a bit of that fear, but the light of day had hastened some of that feeling away.

"Well, what is it?" Zeke asked.

"I don't know," Devon responded. "But do you want to know the scariest part? Zeke nodded his head. "The scariest part was that it kept talking to me...kept asking me questions."

"What kind of questions?" Zeke asked.

"Kept asking me where I was. It kept saying 'come and play, come and play. The water's fine' and, 'the darkness is so soothing,' over and over. And it was in this real low hissing voice...it was..." he said, taking the paper from Zeke and pushing it back under the notebook, "it was...", and then he seemed to ponder for a moment, trying to figure out the best word. Then, as if a small light were lit in his mind, he responded with, "horrific."

* * * * *

For a moment Zeke considered Devon's use of the word "horrific", *Kind of a big word for a twelve year old*, he thought. Then he remembered that Devon was a smart kid, despite his mischievous side. He was always reading and always looking things up on the internet and flipping through the dictionary.

Kinda' nerdy Zeke thought, but that was Devon for you. And then, as if the idea had come out of nowhere Zeke said, "you know what, why don't you bring that drawing with you today, you never know, it might come in handy...you know, in case we have nothing to talk about with Taylre." Then he laughed to himself, wondering if it was even possible that Taylre would have nothing to say. "We can bring it out as a good conversation piece, something we can get a good laugh over."

Devon seemed to consider the idea for just a brief moment, shrugged his shoulders and then reached for the paper, folding it tightly and sticking it in the front pocket of his jeans.

Zeke and Devon tried to make their way quietly down the stairs, when softly, but unexpectedly, the door to their parents' bedroom opened, its creaking hinges moaning their displeasures as if they too were being forced to awaken before their time. Mr. Proper stood at the door, his hair sticking up, his face unshaven and a confused but sleepy look in his eyes. "What are you guys doing? It's not even seven o'clock in the morning."

"We're going to go hang out with Taylre," Zeke whispered.

"Yeah, but don't you think she'll still be asleep? I mean, it is kind of early, don't you think?" he said, rubbing at his swollen eyes and trying in vain to pat down a raised bit of uncombed hair that stuck out stubbornly from the side of his head.

"She's standing outside on the front lawn," Zeke responded.

For a moment, Mr. Proper said nothing. He had seen Taylre for the first time the night before but had heard about her from other relatives, so he seemed to comprehend the situation. Emitting an exasperated sigh, he shook his head with a seemingly distant resignation, gave a slight wave with his hand, and then returned to his room, closing the door gently behind him.

The two boys continued down the stairs. Rufus stood at the bottom of the steps, his tail wagging, anticipating his own exploration of the town. They opened the door and all three of them ran to meet Taylre who was waiting patiently on the sidewalk in front of the house.

"It's about time you guys got here. I thought for a moment there I was going to have to come in and get you," she said, still smiling and still pleasant. "Well, what do you say to going and getting some breakfast?" and this was not a question, really, because Taylre didn't wait for a response. Instead, she just turned herself toward the main part of town and began walking. The two boys looked at each other, shrugged their shoulders and ran to keep up; talking Zeke and Devon into eating would never be an issue.

* * * * *

From the upstairs master bedroom window, Percy Proper stared down at the small group of children who excitedly ran across the street heading toward the center of town. From behind him came the soft breathing of his sleeping wife as she lay curled up in the warmth of the cozy down comforter that enveloped her and her dreams. He turned to look on her resting form and hoped, for the sake of this woman that he loved, and for the sake of the two boys who produced so much energy and joy into his life, that he was doing the right thing. He sat down heavily on the corner of the bed jostling it slightly, but not enough to wake Vivian Proper. Then from him came the leaden sigh of a man who is weighted down with too many cares, too many worries, and too much responsibility. *Nevertheless*, he thought, *it is what it is. It is my fate and I am destined to follow the road that has been chosen for me. I pray that it will all end soon.*

CHAPTER 4

The Captain

This particular morning had a slight crispness in the air, as if winter were right around the corner, though summer had just started. While the four explorers made their way toward the center of town, their breath was visible with each expiration. Zeke and Devon both kept their arms crossed over their chest, patting themselves occasionally, trying in vain to keep themselves warm from the chill in the air, wishing they had put on a sweatshirt over their thin t-shirts. Taylre, even though she was dressed in her typical short overalls and t-shirt, seemed unaffected by the coolness. Perhaps it was the pace that she was able to keep up, her long legs doubling the normal stride of Zeke and Devon's.

The small group rounded a corner and turned onto Main Street. Looking down the length of the street, one could see that it was very much like any other coastal town. On one side, the sea-side, cafes, fish and tackle shops and gift shops lined the street. Behind these was the bay, Gonzales Bay, where docks and marinas hosted a myriad of fishing vessels and pleasure crafts. The skies here were filled with the squabbling cacophony of seagulls. On the other side of Main Street, directly across from the sea-side, were shops galore: dress shops, men's clothing stores, a small movie theatre, restaurants, antique shops, more gift shops (since Alder Cove was a popular tourist stop in the summer time) and of course the Town Hall where the Mayor kept his office.

Taylre lead her followers across Main Street over to the sea-side where they stood before a small café called "Typhoon Jacks". On the window, painted in bright neon colors, were the words:

The best darn breakfast you'll ever eat!

Zeke and Devon glanced at each other, a slight smile on each of their faces. Devon leaned down and patted Rufus tenderly on the head, saying, "Stay boy," while he gently tied a leash around his neck and tied the other end to a rusted bicycle rack. Rufus looked up imploringly with rounded, sad looking eyes, begging to join them in the café.

When they opened the door, they were struck with a most pleasant aroma. From inside came the smells of sizzling sausage and bacon, eggs cooked in butter, pancakes smothered in sticky sweet syrup, crab cakes pan fried in delectable seasonings, deep fried oysters, steamed clams and fresh baked bread. Zeke inhaled the aroma of food with the fervor of a starving man, his head swimming with the blend of smells, making his mouth water. Suddenly, he realized he had no money, neither did Devon. Their dad had given them their allowance just before they began the move to Alder Cove. Unfortunately, they had spent that money on junk food for the long trip. Zeke now began to worry, he didn't want to look like a fool in front of Taylre, and he certainly did not want to have to wash dishes to pay for the meal.

They moved toward the counter and sat on high cushioned stools that swiveled. Devon caught on quickly to the way the stools rotated and began spinning himself round and round until he was dizzy. Zeke sidled up next to Taylre, still wrestling with the fact that he had no money, and whispered softly but urgently to her so that the rather large and mean looking cook behind the counter wouldn't hear, "Taylre...um...this might be a bad time to mention this, but we don't have any money to pay for breakfast."

Taylre turned in her seat, grinning widely, the braces on her teeth glistening brightly. "Have no fear," she said cheerfully, "today is my treat. Just don't get used to it."

From the kitchen, the mean looking bulky cook lumbered up to the counter. When Zeke saw him up close, he gasped inwardly. For one thing he had never seen a man with that big of a head before. *It's enormous*, Zeke thought. *I don't think they make hats that big.*

The man's head was shaved completely bald. His face was already covered in what appeared to be a five-o'clock shadow, even though he had shaved just that morning. His mouth was turned down into a permanent frown, and his chin, well, he didn't really have a chin, just an enormous head going directly into a neck. His shirtsleeves were rolled up his large muscular arms to just below his elbows where a colorful tattoo of a large eel wrapped around an anchor rested tamely on his hairy forearm. The collar of his shirt was deeply stained; as for the pattern on his shirt, Zeke wasn't sure if it was supposed to be there, or if it had been splattered there from some kitchen malfunction.

The man wore an apron that covered his substantial belly; it too was stained with all manner of food and grease. When he spoke, his voice was deep and gravelly, like someone who had smoked a tobacco pipe for most of their life. In addition, when he addressed the trio, he sounded, at least Zeke thought, like a pirate from one of those famous swashbuckler movies. "Well," he grunted, the sound coming from some deep recess of his throat, "It be som' at early for ya youngans to be out, is it not?"

"Aye, captain," Taylre responded cheerily.

The captain eyed the three warily, looking steadily at each child in turn, and then finally resting his sights on Zeke who cringed in his seat. He was terrified of this man. Zeke imagined, for just a brief moment, the Captain taking Zeke's head between his two beefy hands and easily crushing his skull. Then the Captain smiled, not much, but just a little, and it was genuine, a twinkle of laughter in his eyes.

"And you must be a Proper, are ye not? Why I'd bet me life on it." Then he laughed; a deep throated hearty laugh that made both Zeke and Devon giggle in spite of their fear.

Zeke then stopped his laughter abruptly. "How do you know my name?" he asked, his manner concerned, yet curious at the same time.

"Yer name? Why ye look the spittin' image of your gran' da ya do. A great friend he was, a great friend." The Captain turned then, raising his fist to his mouth and bending slightly at the waist he began to cough, steadying himself with the other hand on the counter. The trio, as if by some invisible command, all leaned back on their stools at the same time, trying to avoid any flying spit - or anything else that might be expelled from the Captain's lungs.

Finally, after a few moments of choking, wheezing and spitting, the Captain stood erect, wiped his mouth with the back of his hand and dabbed his forehead with a damp cloth. Zeke, Devon and Taylre resumed their positions at the counter. Zeke, hesitating for just a moment to see if the Captain was through with his coughing fit, asked, "You knew my grandpa?"

"Aye. Joseph and I used to run around in our younger days. He and I owned a fishing boat together. Tried to make a business of it, we did, but the sea took him, you might say. 'Twas a bad day that ware. He left a poor widow behind, and a wee baby - I'm guessin' that'd be yer da."

Zeke nodded, remembering the stories his dad told him about his grandfather. He also remembered the stories he was told of his grandmother's struggles as she tried to raise a small family without a husband. "Yes...I mean, aye, Captain."

There was a brief moment of uncomfortable silence as the solemn thought of a tragic death passed between the small group. Then the Captain cleared his throat, "Well, enough of this," he said, smacking his hand lightly on the counter top. "Yer came to eat, did ya not? So eat is what we'll do. The heavens know thar hasn't been enough customers lately, what, with the dark change and all. So sit up close and get ready for the feast of yer young lives." Then with a flourish, the Captain swung around to the kitchen and began to chop onions, crack open eggs and pour pancake batter, all the while humming a loud ditty.

Zeke, however, noticed none of this. His mind had focused on something the Captain had said, something about the "dark change". He thought of his dad from the day before and how his whole mood had suddenly altered when they came in sight of Alder Cove. *Yeah,* he thought, *that was kind of a "dark change". Is that what the Captain means?* Then, like the alluring call of a siren, the drifting aroma of sizzling bacon recaptured Zeke's thoughts bringing him back to the present with the anticipation of a breakfast feast.

CHAPTER 5

The Yarn

Devon lay curled up on the soft red cushions of a nearby booth in the café, his body concealed behind a table. Soft snores were spilled from his slightly open mouth. Since the restaurant was empty except for Taylre, Zeke and the Captain, no one seemed to mind that Devon had chosen to snooze after the big breakfast.

He's probably exhausted from his lack of sleep last night, thought Zeke. *A little nap will do him good. Maybe even keep him out of my hair for a few moments.* Zeke set down his fork and knife and then took in a deep breath, letting it out slowly. He couldn't remember a time when he had eaten so much food. But, it had tasted so good, just as the Captain said it would, and now, looking down at his distended stomach and feeling a bit of an ache coming on, he was sorry he didn't stop himself after the first helping.

He turned to Taylre who had not said a word the entire time they were eating and noticed that she was now on her third helping of hash browns, crab cakes and sausages. He was amazed at her ability to eat, just as he was with her ability to run. She held onto her fork firmly, as if someone might try to come up and grab it away from her. But she seemed content, and there was no sense in disturbing a person when they were enjoying themselves as much as Taylre obviously was.

He looked into the kitchen where the Captain was scrubbing some pots and scraping accumulated grease and grime from the grill. The Captain looked up from his work and noticed Zeke's attentive stare. Zeke looked away quickly as if he had been suddenly caught doing something he shouldn't. The Captain put down his scraper and walked back to the counter. He stood for a moment watching Taylre enjoy the last of the food on her plate; mopping every drop of syrup off with the remains of a piece of toast. He smiled warmly, obviously basking in the pleasure of watching someone appreciate his cooking as much as he did. He then looked at Zeke, frowning for a moment at his empty plate. "Did ya get enough? There's more to be had if yer willin'."

Zeke shook his head and patted his stomach gently. "Oh no, if I eat another bite I will burst for sure."

Taylre, finally finished with her meal, pushed her plate away and released a loud burp. Zeke looked shocked, his eyes wide and his mouth hanging open. The Captain just laughed, his whole body shaking. "Just like yer Uncle John ye are. Always lettin' the cook know he'd done 'im right with the vittles by lettin' out a great belch, he did." He continued to laugh while he held onto his great belly as if it were going to shake itself off. "And don't look so surprised, lad," he said, looking now at Zeke. "It's just the way to say thankya to the cook, that's all." Then he grabbed the plate and the rest of the dirty dishes that remained on the counter and returned them to the kitchen, tossing them in the soapy water in the sink.

While the Captain lumbered back to the counter, Taylre reached into the front pocket on her bib overalls to retrieve her wallet. She pulled it out and began counting out money from its contents. The Captain, noticing the fanned out display of bills on the counter, frowned disapprovingly. "Nay, we shan't be havin' any of that. This is my treat for ya." Then he pushed the money back toward Taylre.

"But I always pay for my meals here," she responded.

"Not today ye won't. Today is my gift to yas. Besides, there'd hardly been a customer for days now so it don't matter much."

Meanwhile, Devon began to stir on the soft cushioned bench. He sat up quickly, nearly smacking his head on the table in front of him. As he rose, Zeke noted his pale expression. He seemed confused and frightened. "What's going on?" he asked, rubbing sleep from his eyes.

Zeke leaped off his stool and walked over to Devon, gently placing his hand on Devon's shoulder. To Zeke, this seemed like a foreign thing to do. Holding on to Devon like he was a little child and calming him as if he were his father, struck Zeke as odd considering all of the arguing and fighting the two brothers always seemed to be engaged in. Nevertheless, Zeke felt a moment of compassion for his brother, as if he now needed to protect him somehow. "You're okay, buddy. We're here in the café with Taylre and the Captain. You just fell asleep. "

"Where's mom?" he asked, sobbing slightly.

"She's at home, Devon." Zeke said, "tell me what's wrong. Did you have another dream?" Zeke sat down beside his brother and held him like his mom or dad would, rocking him back and forth.

Seeing the concern on Zeke's face and the confusion exhibited by Devon, both Taylre and the Captain moved up next to the brothers. They too were concerned and wanted in some way to offer their help.

Devon's sobbing lessened as he seemed to regain his bearings. He then looked up at Zeke with a fearful gaze, his eyes wide and slightly glazed over. "I saw that thing again - it seemed so real."

The captain bent down now and faced the boy, "What be the problem, lad? Did yer belly get too full?"

"No," Devon answered, shaking his head emphatically. "I had a bad dream...I think."

"A bad dream? Well that's all it is then, just a dream, nothing to be a feared of," the Captain soothed.

"I know," Devon agreed, "I've had dreams before, but this one was different."

"Different, different how?" Taylre chimed in.

"Well, there was this..." and then he remembered the folded up drawing he had in his pocket.

He pulled out the scrap of paper, now badly creased, and opened it onto the table in front of him. The Captain reached for it first, examining the page intently, his bushy eyebrows raising slightly, but the appearance of his face showing a blank expression.

"This thing that you've drawn here, where have ya seen this?" The Captain asked, his tone sounding annoyed and impatient.

"In my dream," Devon responded.

"In yer dream?"

"Aye, Captain," Devon said, eyeing the him with a most serious expression.

"Only in yer dream? You've never seen this thing before in a picture book or in a movie or something like that?" the Captain repeated.

Devon paused for a moment and Zeke turned to look at the Captain wondering why he was asking these questions.

"No..." another pause, " only in my dream."

The Captain nodded his head slowly, implying that he believed Devon and then said, "All of ya, follow me." His tone this time was abrupt and filled with a tense anger that sent a chill up and down Zeke's back.

The Captain walked briskly over to the front door and saw Rufus sitting patiently outside, his leash tied snuggly to an old bike rack.

"Would this be yer dog?" the Captain asked Zeke, his voice returning to its former jolly manner.

"Aye, Captain," Zeke replied.

The Captain stepped out and released the knot on the leash and Rufus eagerly entered the café, his eyes wide with anticipation and his nose working overtime sniffing the air of its diminishing breakfast aromas. The Captain closed the door and turned the latch to lock it. Then he spun around the "open" sign to "closed". He turned and headed straight for the kitchen and out through the back door. The kids followed closely behind.

As the group exited the café, each in turn began to shade their eyes from the sun that had now risen, chasing the chill from the air. The Captain continued to lead them toward the wharf and the many idle fishing boats resting at their berths. He guided them quickly along the floating docks, seemingly intent upon a certain boat that also stood idle, docked along side the pier. When they reached the boat, Zeke could see that it had been well used, on its last legs, actually, was the phrase that first came to his mind. He wondered if this was the same boat that both the Captain and his grandfather had owned together. The same one that his grandfather was on when he had lost his life to the sea.

"Come aboard, then," the Captain said. "Watch yer don't slip on the bird poop, that stuff'll get yer every time, especially the fresh drops. And watch yer head that yer don't bump it goin' down into the galley."

Then Taylre, Zeke, and Devon leaped over the side of the boat in turn, easily finding footing on the deck of the boat, whereas the Captain strained to heave his bulk over the side. Meanwhile, Rufus was barking frantically, trying to lift himself over the side and onto the boat. However, as Devon turned to assist Rufus, the dog's attention was distracted by a noisy flock of seagulls which had perched themselves on another section of dock. Rufus went running after them, apparently all former thoughts of wanting to join his companions gone.

"Oh well," Devon said, shrugging his shoulders as he watched the dog run off. "He knows where we are. He'll be back." And with that, he turned and continued to follow the others down into the belly of the boat.

The steps leading to the bottom of the boat were steep, and a dank odor rose from below, produced from the murky, brackish water that sloshed around in the corners. The Captain, Zeke thought, moved surprisingly well considering the small rolling movements of the boat and the size of the Captain himself. Evidently, years at sea had strengthened his sea legs.

When the small group reached the bottom, they found that space was tight and that any kind of movement was severely limited. Zeke located a small three legged stool and offered it to Taylre which she accepted gladly, her braces glistening along with her smile. Devon found an empty wooden box that smelled of long dead fish. He tipped it over and sat, motioning for Zeke to join him on the narrow platform. Meanwhile, the

Captain stood before an old wooden chest, pulling at its rusted lock. The lock, it seemed, did not need a key, since the Captain appeared to be intent upon tugging at it to get it open. After a few more violent jerks, the lock finally came free and the lid opened.

The trio, as if pulled by some invisible strings, leaned forward, curious as to the contents of the trunk. Their view, however, was blocked by the Captain's enormous girth who stood with his back to the small assemblage. He bent down, reached into the trunk, and pulled out a large leather bound book. Its covering was faded and cracked with age, and small mounds of accumulated dust slid off the top as the Captain tilted it and began to open its heavy lid-like cover.

"This," he said proudly, turning to face the children, "is a very old, very valuable book. Not many have laid eyes upon it as you have today. Consider yer'selves lucky to be witness to it." He gently laid the book upon a small eating table and carefully, almost lovingly, opened its yellowed pages.

The three onlookers inched themselves forward so that their butts were perched on the edges of their seats. They gazed hungrily at the book, as if the manuscript itself held some sort of magic. They appeared mesmerized by the way the Captain turned the pages, like a man searching for a lost diamond among a room filled with delicate crystal. Finally, the Captain located whatever he was searching for and laid the page open, turning the entire book slowly around so that the three cousins could easily view its contents. When both Zeke and Devon saw the large illustration, they gasped inwardly, both of them covering their mouths in an effort to stifle a scream. But instead of screaming, Devon laughed uncomfortably. Not because he saw the illustration as amusing, but because he felt a very cruel joke had just been played upon him. Laughter, he thought, was the only way to battle this kind of cruelty. Neither Zeke nor Taylre said anything; they just stared in wonder. For on the page before them was a picture, the same picture that Devon had drawn on his crumpled up piece of paper. Yet this drawing remained more vivid, larger than life almost. The faded colors of the artwork leapt off the page in some sort of evil dance macabre.

"What you see before ye is *Korrigan,*" the Captain explained. " Or as some call her, *The Washer-Woman.* This," the Captain emphasized by pointing and resting his finger heavily upon the page, "is *not real.* Do ya hear what I'm tellin' ya? It's not real. It's only a myth, a legend. Don't let anyone tell ya otherwise."

There was then a moment of uncomfortable silence as six pair of eyes continued to stare. Zeke finally broke the hushed tenseness, clearing his throat before he spoke. "No one is suggesting it's real," Zeke said timidly. "We're all just a little surprised by the resemblance of this picture to the one that Devon drew. The one he dreamt about." Then, as kind of an after thought, Zeke said, "And why a Washer-Woman? Why would someone think to call this thing a woman at all? There's no way this thing even remotely resembles a woman, at least not one that I've ever seen."

"I know," the Captain answered. "But thar was a time long before electric washin' machines and such when women used to clean the laundry at the edge of the river, slapping the clothes on flat rocks. That way they could beat the dirt and filth out of them. When the *Korrigan* gets hold of her victims, she kills them first on the flat rocks, smashing their brains out before she takes a bite. That's why folks called her the washer-woman; she kills her prey just like a woman beating the filth from a bag of laundry."

The captain seemed annoyed again, as if he had been through this before and had no intention of reliving it or retelling it. Then he added, "they'll be some who'll try to tell you that thar be some sort of magic about it; some sort of hocus-pocus. But I'm here to tell ya that thar isn't. Not one bit."

He sat down heavily on a cushioned chair and began rubbing his whiskery chin with his thumb and forefinger. He was contemplative as the three children sat quietly and uneasily across from him. Finally, Taylre sat forward, resting her knobby elbows on the open book. "Captain," she said. "Who will try to tell us that there's magic? What is it that you're not telling us?"

The Captain took in a deep breath and shook his head in defeat. "Well," he said. "I suppose it's best that it come from me and not someone else. And I suppose you'd be hearin' it soon enough anyway. So, I'll tell ya. But I want ya'll to understand that it's all nothin' but fish guts - not good for anything but catchin' crabs, ya hear?" The trio nodded their heads in unison. Then Zeke, considering once again the Captain's words about a *dark change,* hoped that now some questions would be answered.

"There's a legend," the Captain began. "Of a people that used to inhabit this land."

"The Indians!" Devon shouted enthusiastically.

"No, not the Indians, lad. People who lived here long before thar was any Indians, or Christopher Columbus, or Pilgrims, or any of that. No, I'm talkin' about people who used to live here one, maybe two thousand years ago, longer even. Nobody really knows for sure. Anyways, these people were known simply as the People from the North. They came from far across the ocean it's said. Came across in boats that could ride o' top of the water and under it if need be. Some say the boats were built like giant dishes with a lid on top to keep everybody inside dry and warm.

"The legend says that they left thar homes, the land of thar birth, because thar was no more food. Apparently, thar bein' some kind of famine. The sun got too hot and the rains stopped comin'. People who lived in this far off place began to fight amongst themselves. Each person trying to kill the other for food. Families were divided and great cities fell. However, there was a small group of people, families that stuck together, ya see. Rode out the storm ya might say. They decided to leave the mess, to getaway from the fightin' and death. So, they left. Small groups of them in seven or eight of those dish boats I was talkin' about. Men, women and children.

"They traveled for many days, weeks, even months. Riding over the giant waves, and being pushed by the wind."

"But food. And light. It must have been awfully dark in those boats, what did they do about that?" Zeke inquired.

"I guess they brought enough food with them, as much as they could find, and they packed it all inside. And, as the legend says, they had glowing rocks. Rocks, the books say that were lit by the hand of Odin, the great god of the North folk. Legend has it that this Odin suffered many days in order to obtain the secrets of those stones - these secrets were passed on to mankind. These North Folk were the recipients of those secrets, and they guarded those mysteries well. They were a superstitious group of people believing in rituals, ceremonies and sacrifices. These glowing rocks are what kept it all alight inside when the lids were on."

"Glowing stones?" Taylre exclaimed. "I've never heard of anything like that."

"Well, I told ya, it's only a story isn't it. A fable to tell around a warm fire, or a yarn to keep the sailors up at night on a long watch." The Captain reached for his pipe and stuffed the end with tobacco. He struck a match and held it close to the dark fragrant leaves until they began to glow red. A column of gray smoke began to drift from the corners of the Captain's mouth as he closed the pouch of tobacco and stuffed it back inside his coat pocket, puffing gently on the tip of the pipe. "Now, where was I," he continued.

"Stones," Zeke said.

"Eh?" the Captain retorted.

"Stones. You were talking about the glowing stones in the boat."

"Oh," he grunted. "So I was. Well, anyways, they made it across, you see. Made it across and landed not far from here. When they got to shore they immediately started to build homes, plant crops and set up a small town.

"As time went on the people started to have babies..." the Captain turned an embarrassed red in the cheeks. "Now, I don't need to go into that do I?" The others shook their heads. No need, they already knew where babies came from. "Well good," he said, taking a quick, deep breath.

"Having babies meant there were more and more people. Soon, according to the legend, this whole area became filled with people. This whole coastline and all up in the hills west of here was covered with cities...people all over the place. Why they say thar be near a million folks livin' in this very place some four thousand year ago. Can ya believe that? No, I can't either," the Captain could see the trio shaking their heads.

"But what happened to them?" Zeke asked. "If there were supposed to be that many people, wouldn't there be some kind of sign that they were here? Wouldn't there be at least some old ruined buildings?"

"A good question lad. Some say thar be some ruins here about, places not many people venture up to. They say the regions far back in the woods are haunted or some such nonsense. Which is exactly why I say the story isn't nothing' but fish bait."

"Okay," Taylre said. "Let's suppose there were some people who used to live here. What happened to them?"

"Another good question lass. And here be the answer: The old book here says it war' famine. Yes, another famine. Just like the one that sent 'em packin' in the first place. However, this one, at least according to the legend, was worse than the one they originally fled from. The whole area dried up. No crops, no fish, no nothin'. It got so bad that people were dyin off left and right. They were fightin' amongst themselves for even the smallest morsel of food. Men and women would kill their own children to have something to eat. It was terrible."

"So, that's what happened? They all died of starvation?" Zeke said incredulously.

"Well, not quite," the Captain answered. "You remember I told ya' before that they were a superstitious people?" Again, the unified nodding of heads. "Well there were a few left who worked in the dark ways. In other words, they practiced black magic, and with these evil skills they decided to conjure up a remedy for their famine problem. And that, my three youngins', is where this comes in." He pointed again with a stern finger at the hideous picture of Korrigan.

"You mean to say that this Korrigan, this Washer-woman, was their cure for the famine?" Zeke questioned.

"That's right lad. The legend says that the mischievous Loki, the devil himself, controls the sea, and that it were him that spawned this demon. It was him who sent the creature after the people did their evil ritual."

"Are you saying that this thing came from the sea?" Devon asked.

"Aye lad. Came from the sea, crawled its putrid, filthy body up on the shore, and then stumbled on its awkward legs up into the hills to wait."

"Wait?" Zeke said. "Wait for what?"

"Dinner," the Captain exclaimed. "A thing like that has to be fed. And that is exactly what the dirty Northerns did; they fed it. They had to. In order to keep up their end of the bargain...the Korrigan would keep the famine away as long as it was fed."

"So you're saying that all they had to do was feed the thing and the famine would go away? Well, that doesn't sound so bad," Zeke said.

"Aye, lad. But this stinkin' Korrigan had a special diet, and only one thing could appease its hunger: a human."

"So these people from the north, they made a human sacrifice?" Taylre asked skeptically.

"That's right lass. A human sacrifice to keep the monster happy. But that's not all. When the beast was finally fed with the right sacrifice, it would return to the sea, thankfully, but it would come back every thirty-year or so expecting its human offering. If it didn't get it, the people would suffer again. Famine would return. The fish would dry up and the rain would stop. A cloud of misery would hover over the land like a solar eclipse, sendin' folks into a dark mood of depression and despair."

"And would they?" Devon asked. "Would they keep on feeding it...make sacrifices to it, I mean?"

"Aye, so they say."

"Who?" Devon continued. "Who would they use? For the sacrifice."

"Ah, well now, that is the most interesting question of them all." The Captain leaned forward, his pudgy hand smoothing the surface of the large book in front of him as he lowered his voice to an almost inaudible whisper. "It be said that the meal, the sacrifice, must be from a worthy line. From a family with strong deep roots. The book itself, if ya believe in such things, says this," and then he turned the pages of the ancient text slowly until he found the right spot. Then he began to read.

> *Adrift,*
> *Alone, the sea will send*
> *A demon to appease.*
> *A ransom strong*
> *And lifted up*
> *Is all that's asked to please*
>
> *The ransomed gift will scribe his thoughts*
> *For souls of men to speak.*
> *An image of the past he'll tell*
> *Of hands that seek in need.*
>
> *Willingly he must employ*
> *His duty to the clan,*
> *Else famine, death and pestilence*
> *Will clamber in the land.*

"I don't get it," Devon said. "Is that supposed to be some sort of clue or something?"

The Captain shook his head, "All I know is that thar have been times when things have gotten out of hand. When things that should have been left as nonsense have been taken literally, like this verse here. When that happens, people get hurt. Or worse, they get killed."

"Wait, wait," Zeke exclaimed. "If I'm hearing you right you're saying that there are people around that might still *believe* in this Korrigan. That might think that the reason things are slow in Alder Cove this summer is because of this, this demon? That they somehow think it's returned or something?"

The Captain took in another slow, deep breath. He shifted in his seat and took another short puff on his pipe. "What I'm sayin' lad, is that thar be some folks here that are still mighty superstitious. Folks who believe in some pretty outlandish things. But I'm here to tell ya that they're not true, and to not go belivin' in em'. That's all." With that he closed up the great book with the faded image of the demon and placed it gently back in his wooden trunk.

CHAPTER 6

Encounter

The Stick River emptied into the ocean just south of the town of Alder Cove. It was a slow moving river that was narrow but very deep. It would have made a good route for smaller watercraft because of its depth and its narrow width, but for some odd reason boaters refused to venture upstream. Thus, the banks of the river for miles along remained free of buildings or docks. The river meandered unchallenged through open fields up into the hills surrounding the town and then finally toward its headwaters somewhere high up in the coastal range where winter snows and small springs fed it.

For most of its length, the Stick River parted its way through privately owned land. The fields on one side of the river were usually filled with healthy grazing cattle chewing happily on thick, full grass. On the opposite side of the river, fertile fields would sprout hearty crops that the owners of the land could sell for a plentiful profit. Now, though, the crops withered in the dried, cracked ground. In addition, the cattle sought in vain for greenery to graze upon, their rib bones visibly rubbing up against the insides of their flesh, displaying the famine-like conditions that seemed to encompass the area.

The coastal highway dipped and turned, rose and fell, sometimes violently twisting its way across the Stick River on an old wooden bridge, which creaked when oversized trucks passed. It was underneath this bridge that Ramon and Terrance sat, shaded from the heat of the sun, their fishing rods perched on their laps, the lines leading into the depths of the deep green waters as the boys waited impatiently for a bite.

"Anything?" Ramon asked, knowing the answer to his question before he asked it, but feeling the weight of the silence too much to bear.

"Nothing, you?" Terrance responded, pulling off his glasses and cleaning them gently on the sleeve of his shirt.

"Naw, not even a nibble. I'm beginning to think there are no fish in this river."

Terrance placed his glasses back on his face. "Oh there's fish alright," he said. "Last summer my dad caught a huge salmon from this very spot. In fact, I think we still have some of it in the freezer at home. It was a beauty!"

"Were you with him when he caught it?" Ramon asked.

"No. He caught it while we were at school."

"Well, there ya go."

"Whadya mean?"

"I mean your old man never caught a fish from here. He just told ya that to make himself look good. You know, like the big bad hunter comin' home with the food for the family." Ramon grinned, knowing this conversation would start to bug him.

Terrance looked over at Ramon, his eyes narrowing at the accusation that his own father would lie. "Alright smart guy, so where did my dad get the fish? Whadya think, he just made it out of Lego or something?"

Ramon laughed. Egging on Terrance was always so easy. "No, Einstein, he bought it from the grocery store, thawed it out and then brought it home sayin' he caught it here. Dads do that kind of stuff all the time."

Terrance shook his head. He was not going to let Ramon raze him this time. "Maybe your dad does, but not mine. He caught it right out of this river, from the very spot that we are sittin' at right now."

"Whatever," Ramon said, winding his line, making a barely audible click. "All I know is that we've been sittin' here for over two hours with nothing. No bite, no nibble, not even a fish fart, and I'm tired of waitin'." He stood, his lure now secure and his tackle box in hand.

"So, you're giving up?" Terrance began to reel in his line as well.

"For today. Maybe we can come back tomorrow."

"So, what do we do in the meantime? And don't say go back to your house to play video games. I'm getting sick of those."

Ramon turned and looked upstream, his eyes focusing on the fields that edged the river and then the distant copse of trees that stood like sentinels at the base of the foothills. He turned to Terrance, "let's go over there," he said, pointing to the trees.

"What, are you mental?" Terrance began to number off with his fingers. "One, that's all private land, we'd be trespassing. Two, that's kind of a long hike, and three, that's…" he paused, his three fingers held out like shields against evil.

" What? What were you going to say?" Ramon asked, an impish grin forming on his lips.

"Nothing," Terrance sheepishly responded.

"Yes you were," Ramon insisted. "You were going to say… haunted," he said, letting the word hang like a sharp and jagged icicle.

Terrance said nothing, but his eyes darted toward the trees and a shiver rose up his neck, standing the small blond hairs on end. His feet shifted nervously in the gravel, the toe of his shoe boring a small hole in the hardened river bank. Finally, he responded, his voice a slight whisper, "my dad said..."

Ramon groaned, "Your dad said what? That the boogieman lives there. Give me a break! Next you're going to tell me that Jack has a beanstalk there too."

"I'm just telling you what I've heard, Ramon. Nobody goes there. Nobody. Haven't you ever wondered why nobody ever goes there?"

"Yeah, I have wondered that. That is exactly why we should go there, to prove everybody wrong. To show everybody that the place isn't haunted and that all of the old fogies around here are nothing but a bunch of superstitious dorks."

Terrance considered this for a moment but held on tentatively to the old fear that he still felt. "I don't know," he said, gesturing stiffly with his arm toward the overgrown path that lead along the edge of the river. "The path is pretty faded and it's kinda' hot out. We might be walking for a long time."

"Not a problem," Ramon responded enthusiastically, seeing that his coaxing was working. "We'll just stay along the edge of the river, there's no way we can get lost, and I've got plenty of water in my Camel Back. Also, I have Power bars in my tackle box. See, we're set. It shouldn't take us more than an hour to get there. Whadya' say?"

Terrance continued to look toward the distant hills, his features softening a little. "Okay," he said finally. "We'll hike until we get to the trees, then we head back. And..." he continued. "Any sign of trouble, we scram, and not the way we came, but across the fields toward town. If we go back the way we came we'll be there for hours. Agreed?"

"Agreed," Ramon said, turning quickly and heading up the faded path, hoping Terrance wouldn't change his mind.

* * * * *

The boys had been walking on a steady incline for over an hour, always keeping to the edge of the river. Terrance's former apprehension of joining the hike in the first place was worsening. He worried that he wouldn't reach home before dark, and the light was beginning to fade. However, what made matters worse was the fact that they had already passed at least a half dozen **"DO NOT ENTER"**, or **"DANGER-NO TRESPASSING"** signs. He imagined that if they weren't careful they would both be spending the night in the county jail.

They started on a dead path that was practically invisible. Weeds and tall grass took over along the edge of the river; Ramon and Terrance struggled to keep pace as they continued toward their goal of reaching the thicket of trees.

"Ramon, this is crazy. Let's turn back," Terrance said.

"Are you nuts? We're almost there. Besides, you agreed to go as far as the trees."

"Yeah, but that was before I realized we'd be on an all day hike," he responded, sitting down in the tall grass to take off his shoe. He shook the worn canvas high top vigorously and a small pebble dropped to the ground.

"Look," Ramon pointed toward the closest tree. "Another ten minutes and we'll be there. We'll walk around a bit and then leave."

Terrance reluctantly stood up, brushed the dirt off the front of his pants and walked passed Ramon, his face set in anger; he realized it was futile to argue with Ramon, just continue and get the thing over with.

The boys continued to walk for another third of a mile with Ramon leading the march. They had just entered the first of the lower, smaller trees that stood at the outer tip of the dense trees when Ramon stopped abruptly, kneeled down in the shorter, dried grass, and began smoothing the palm of his hand over the surface of the ground. "Hey, check this out," he said, urging Terrance over with the wave of his hand.

Terrance knelt down beside Ramon, his attention drawn to the place where Ramon was brushing dirt away, smoothly, like an archeologist on his first dig. "There," he said. "Look how the rocks are all placed together. Like bricks, but on the ground."

Terrance looked closely, "Yeah, like an English road," he said, now helping to push the thin layer of dirt away.

"A what?"

"An English road. You know, like the ones they used to have in England and the rest of Europe. Cobblestone."

Ramon continued to follow the embedded stones with the palm of his hand, noting that their path lead northerly, toward town, and in the opposite direction, keeping parallel to the river. He noted also that the width of the bricks all lined up together could indeed make up a road, a road that had been there for a very long time.

As he looked up, Terrance still at his side brushing away dirt, he noticed another crumbling stone structure that was partially concealed by overgrown grass, weeds and taller trees.

"Look over here," he said, moving over to the stones and pulling away vines and roots that had grown over the sides. "This looks like a wall. At least part of one."

The structure was about four feet high. It was made entirely from stone, flat on the sides and the top in the shape of a rectangle with an area of approximately 12 feet. Ramon stood on it and tested its strength, then looked around from his new vantage point.

"It's getting dark," he said, noting the fading light, especially where the trees began to thicken and where the receding sun cast ominous shadows.

Terrance had been engrossed in his labor of cleaning away the dirt from the stone road, but at the mention of the fading light looked up, his old fears returning. "Yeah, we'd better go," he stuttered. "I want to get home before dark."

Ramon jumped down from the stones. "Five more minutes, bud, that's all I ask. I want to follow this cobble road for just five more minutes and then we head home, alright?"

Five more minutes. Ten more minutes. When will it stop? Terrance thought. "Alright, five more then we go. In fact, I'm timing it." He looked at the watch on his wrist and pushed some buttons, high-pitched beeps came from his stopwatch. "When this goes off, we leave. Agreed?"

"Agreed," said Ramon, starting again along the river, this time following the cobble stoned path.

The boys had walked for only a few moments when suddenly an overwhelming darkness seemed to fall upon them. Terrance stopped, looked up, confused, seeing that the retreating sun had not yet abandoned the horizon; the sky above was clear. Ramon stopped too, feeling goose bumps appear, raising the tiny hairs on his arms and the intense impression that they were being watched, closely.

Ramon turned to look at Terrance, his back to the river, "Do you feel that?" Ramon asked, his eyes wide with sudden fear.

Terrance tried to swallow, but the saliva in his mouth had become as thick as paste. He could not speak although he tried several times to spit out the words: *I am terrified; something is there, behind you, in the water.* But, only hoarse sounds from the back of his throat managed to escape his mouth.

As Terrance struggled to speak, there suddenly arose a dark form out of the river that loomed like a grizzly shadow behind Ramon. Terrance saw it rise, but could do nothing. It was as if his feet were rooted to the ground upon which he stood.

Ramon saw Terrance's eyes lift to look above his head, and then he felt the presence of an evil so thick that it had the power to bind his tongue so that he too could not speak. An evil invaded his mind where darkness gathered, where no light could enter. Ramon felt at once a combination of emotions: hatred, malice, depression, despair and... murder. Ramon fought the sensation. He struggled against its influence, its captivating grip, but he was losing the battle. Although his mind grappled with the true essence of right and wrong, he could not escape this overwhelming desire.

To murder.

His eyes focused on Terrance.

Terrance saw the expressions on Ramon's face change from fear to horror, to revulsion and then to...what? *Why was Ramon looking at him like that?* His eyes illuminated a faint yellowish glow, and with it an overpowering odor - the smell of rotting flesh, long since discarded on the garbage heap of hell.

Terrance tried again to move, but his fear would not allow it. He tried to speak. To call to Ramon. To tell him, no! To order him to stop, but his voice failed him. Ramon's mouth turned into an angry sneer. His teeth showed through his slightly parted lips and a low growl, oozed from his throat.

The dark, massive creature looming behind Ramon suddenly struck with lightening speed, tearing into the back of Ramon's neck with a crunching sound and lifted him high above the thickened tree line. Ramon continued to look down at Terrance as he was elevated, smiling, as if welcoming the obliteration of his body, his soul.

Finally, with the creature's sudden movement and Ramon's wraithlike look in his eyes, Terrance was able to force his feet to move, to force logic beyond fear. He began moving awkwardly backwards, stumbling slightly on exposed roots and rock but managing to keep his balance. He turned and ran from the river heading toward the town; to safety. He turned once to see Ramon, still in the grasp of the dark creature's jaws, being plummeted from the tree tops, head first, with the force of a sledgehammer. The impact, though hidden behind the high banks of the river, expelling a liquid crunch, like a melon being crushed on asphalt.

CHAPTER 7

Whispers Behind Closed Doors

That night, the officer in charge of the Alder Cove Police Department, Chief Teddy Walford, a man so large he barely fit his circumstances, sat uncomfortably in the driver's seat of his squad car. The engine of the black and white vehicle idled roughly in the parking lot of a small convenience store, jiggling a cup of coffee that sat perched on the officer's expanded belly; his left hand steadying the beverage; his right, balancing a jelly-filled donut that he looked at almost lovingly. He dipped a sugar crusted edge of the donut into the coffee, dripping some of the liquid on his uniform, and stuffed a large portion of it into his mouth, chewing eagerly, making small humming sounds as he ate; his enjoyment of the small meal audible.

The radio on the dashboard suddenly came alive with chatter. Officer Walford reached over to turn up the volume as an anonymous dispatcher's voice reported the discovery of a young teenage boy "acting suspiciously", curled up in the backyard of a local resident. The caller reported that the boy was babbling incoherently.

Chief Walford reluctantly placed his coffee in a cup holder and threw the remaining donut back into a bakery bag. Then forcefully he jammed the transmission into drive. He turned on the car's red flashing lights and muttered under his breath as he drove out of the parking lot, "Kid's probably smoking some drugs."

Zeke, Taylre and Devon stood on the sidewalk outside of the town's small movie theater. Rufus eagerly wagged his tail as

Devon approached and untied his leash from a bicycle rack. The small group came together again and began talking all at once, excitedly rehashing the adventures of the hero in the movie they had just seen. Suddenly, their conversation was interrupted by the sounds of police and ambulance sirens. They turned and watched as the vehicles drove past, their curiosity piqued but not overwhelmed. Rufus howled at the sounds of the passing sirens trying to match their ear piercing pitch, while the trio covered their ears as scant protection from the throbbing sound.

As the emergency vehicles drifted away so did the siren's cry. Rufus ceased his own howling and looked up expectantly at his companions, waiting for the next adventure of the day. Since the interruption of the wailing sirens, the trio remained quiet, all thoughts of the film they had just seen fading into a distant memory; an uncomfortable gloominess clouding their thoughts.

From the time they left the Captain's boat and the morbid discussion about the Korrigan, the three friends had become mute on the subject. No one, it seemed, wanted to bring up the discussion again. They shared a fear that perhaps further dialogue on the matter would cause it to become... what? Real? Something that reached beyond the accepted bounds of their sheltered lives? Taylre reflected in the midst of the dreariness and silence to consider the impact of such a tale, if, in fact, it were true. *A reality like that*, she thought, *would crush the comfort I have always felt in the nonexistence of such fairy tales and myths. There's got to be order to life. The existence of a monster like the Korrigan would stifle that order. No*, she thought, *not in this town. Not in this world. A creature like that can't really exist.* Yet, as she thought this, a sense of fear filled her mind. She turned to see Zeke looking at her. His eyes mirroring a similar look of concern and dread.

"We need to talk," she finally said, breaking the encompassing silence that was left in the absence of the police and ambulance sirens. She stared at the two brothers, and then indicated with the slight shift of her head to the left that they were to follow her. She started out with her usual long strides moving toward Pike Street and home.

Since the time the small troupe had left earlier in the day, heading off first for a large breakfast at Typhoon Jacks, Zeke and Devon had found themselves the recipients of a grand tour of Alder Cove, presented exclusively by Taylre Anders. She led them up and down the piers where they stopped and looked at the various fishing boats, yachts and sailboats. They ran along the rocky beaches at the north end of town where they collected colorful shells, sand dollars and gently poked at starfish and sea anemones with sticks, watching them shrink from the touch. They waded in the tide pools with their shoes and socks off and their pants rolled up, feeling the coolness of the salt water and the sifting of warm sand between their toes.

As lunchtime neared, Taylre, her generosity intact, treated the boys to beer- battered Halibut and coleslaw at a small café where they sat outside on plastic deck chairs, feeling the ocean breeze toss their hair and fill their lungs with refreshment. They laughed and told stories about themselves. Taylre told the boys about the local school they would be attending in the fall and about her own family, how she lost her parents in a car accident and now lived with her grandmother. The boys, in turn, told Taylre about their mom and dad, how they left their home in the city to come and live in Alder Cove. The Mayor, David Vernon, recently offered their dad a job as the new City Planner. It seemed like a perfect opportunity, the boys said; their dad would have a chance to return to his childhood town.

The trio continued throughout the afternoon looking through the various souvenir shops, t-shirt stores and toyshops that lined Main Street. As night approached, the small group decided to see a movie in the one and only movie theater in town. They were pacified by the excitement that the film portrayed and they quickly found themselves lost in the story and the lives of the characters.

It had been a full and active day. All three exhibited a slight redness on their cheeks from the sun and the vibrancy and carelessness of youth. Yet, a deep nagging feeling pulled at them causing their minds to darken; it was only through concentrating on the happiness of the day that caused the darkness to fade and the light to return.

As the companions made their way up the poorly lit streets toward home, Zeke felt the weight of the upcoming conversation that Taylre wanted to have. He did not want to talk about the Captain or his book. He did not want to consider the possibility that there might be something to the story of the Korrigan, but there were too many coincidences, Devon's drawing being the biggest and most disturbing one.

"We've been avoiding this all day, all of us have," Taylre began. "It's time to get this out in the open. We can't deny the feelings we've all been having today. I can tell that we've all had them. I can tell just by looking at both of you."

The brothers nodded in unison. Neither of them could deny what they'd felt, but they remained silent despite Taylre's encouragement to get things out in the open.

Pushing further, Taylre said, "Devon, what do you think? I mean you have the picture. You drew something that looks like the one in the book. Doesn't that bother you?"

Devon looked up in shock. He was hoping to be left out of this discussion. Expressing deep, or even surface feelings was never his strongest trait. He looked to Zeke for help, an unusual request since Devon was usually so confident in himself. However, he could see, with just a glance at Zeke, that no help would come; he was on his own. He shook his head slowly, "I don't know what to say Taylre. Maybe I saw it somewhere before. Maybe it was something I saw on T.V., something that only looked like the thing in the Captain's book. I don't know, I really don't know."

Taylre stopped walking. She hung her long skinny arms in exasperation, her head hung back as she stared into space, sighing. The answer Devon gave her evidently did not meet her approval. Zeke was surprised to see this reaction; so far he had only seen a much lighter side of Taylre.

"What do you want him to say," Zeke said, defending Devon. "This has all been pretty weird, you have to admit. I really don't think there is a definite answer here."

Taylre paused a moment. She brought her eyes forward, breathing deeply, as if to gain her composure, "I know, I'm sorry. I didn't mean to snap. It's just that I've seen some things recently, things that happened before you two came." She moved to the curb at the side of the street and sat down. Zeke and Devon followed suit beside her while Rufus laid his head lovingly on Taylre's lap.

They waited for her to speak further, choosing to remain silent, fearing that speaking to her now would somehow break an imaginary spell that would keep her from talking more.

Taylre stroked Rufus's head absentmindedly then pressed on. "There's something going on in Alder Cove, and I can't quite put my finger on it. There's a feeling, you know, as if nobody trusts anybody anymore. Like everyone is paranoid and afraid to leave their houses. As if there's a...a heaviness. Yeah, like a heaviness, that's it. But you can't see it or, and I know this sounds weird, you can't really feel it either, but it's there all the same."

She looked at the brothers. They stared at her with wide, expectant eyes, willing her to go on, but she only stared back, hoping her words were making some sense, because right now they didn't make much to her.

Zeke finally spoke, breaking the tension of the moment. "You're right, Taylre. It does sound weird, but at the same time I think I kind of know what you're talking about." Devon sat, quietly nodding his own muted agreement.

"Well," she said finally, rising from her cement seat. "We're not solving anything by sitting here. Let's go home and get some rest. It's been a long, busy day. Maybe tomorrow we can make more sense of it all when it's daylight. If you're willing to talk about it that is."

Both Zeke and Devon rose from the curb, rubbing warmth into their now cooled butts, "I'm okay with that," Zeke said, smiling. Then he turned abruptly, just as he'd seen Taylre do, and walked away at a steady pace in the direction of home.

As the friends neared Pike Street, they turned into an alleyway that lead behind some of the older homes that had come to establish Alder Cove as an antique establishment, when they were suddenly blinded by the flashing blue, white and red lights of the emergency vehicles they had first encountered earlier on Main Street.

Curiosity got the best of Taylre, "Come on," she said, beckoning the brothers to follow.

They crossed over the gravel lined alleyway quickly to the right side, kicking up bits of rock as they went. They gathered next to a low chain link fence that surrounded a neighbor's backyard. The enclosure was immaculately manicured. The grass was kept even and short, and the borders of the lawn were crisply edged. Surrounding the enclosure, lining the chain link fence, were various sizes and shapes of expertly tended bushes. Within the confines of the yard the three could see a swarm of police, paramedics and other non-uniformed people all standing around one corner of the yard; their attention drawn to a crouching figure that was huddled in a self embrace under some thickly leaved shrubbery.

Devon nudged Taylre slightly, "What is that?" he asked. "Is it an animal?"

"I'm not sure," she responded. "It's a little too dark to see, but I think it's a boy."

The companions moved along the fence line, sneaking as close as they dared without drawing too much attention to themselves. As they got closer to the gathered group, the mixed sounds of sobbing and stifled shouts assaulted their ears. Among the cries from the curled up form were the gentle coaxing calls of a woman. The three leaned in and were able to discern, just barely, the words that she spoke, "Please, come out honey," she pleaded. "We're all here to help you. Won't you tell us what's wrong?"

The begging continued, but the boy, as it turned out to be, would not leave the confines of his dark corner of the yard. If anyone tried to move in to pull the boy out, he would lash out with his hands and fingers curled into small claws, screaming in terror, as if he were a trapped, terrified wild animal.

Taylre looked on in shocked amazement. "I know that boy," she said. "He goes to my school. His name is Terrance." She covered her mouth, shaking her head in disbelief that a fellow student and acquaintance could be suffering so badly.

"What's wrong with him?" Zeke whispered.

"I don't know," she responded. "He's a good kid. I can't imagine that he's gotten into anything he shouldn't."

Just then, Officer Walford waddled up to the trio, his hand resting on the butt of his revolver. They were startled when he spoke since they were so intent on watching Terrance. "It's a little late for you kids to be out, don't you think? Maybe you three ought to find something better to do with your time. Better yet, why don't ya'll head on home. There's nothing to see here."

The three cowered slightly at the officer's words and turned quickly toward home. Taylre twisted back opening her mouth to speak to the officer, but he simply glared at her as if daring her to ask him the question that was on her mind. Instead, she closed her mouth, an effort she found to be almost overwhelming, and turned to catch up to Zeke and Devon.

The three walked in silence, mulling over the image of Terrance, his terrified eyes and his animal-like intensity. They stopped in front of Taylre's house, seeing that the porch light was on and a number of cars were parked in the driveway and along the front curb. This puzzled Taylre, but made no mention of her concern to either Zeke or Devon. She knelt down and patted Rufus tenderly on the head, scratching lightly behind his ears. When she stood up, she could see that both of the boys had that familiar expectant look in their eyes, as if she were to somehow offer them an explanation for the oddity that they had just witnessed.

"I don't know what you want me to say," she said, responding to their unspoken question. "What we just saw back there indicates the kind of things I was just talking about. There is something weird going on in this town. I think we should just keep to our original plan: go home, get some rest and talk more about it in the morning and hope that the light of day will shed some answers on some of the things we've seen and heard today."

Zeke smiled and nodded, "You're right. We should head home. Maybe tomorrow we can discover more about what's going on. Let's just hope this is all some sort of practical joke that we can all laugh about."

Zeke and Taylre shook hands awkwardly. Taylre then bent down to give Devon a hug, which he reciprocated. She turned and walked to her front porch while the boys dashed to their house across the street. Taylre watched them run up the front steps, push open the big front door and enter. She was glad to see that they were in safely for the night.

"A practical joke would be a welcomed relief," she muttered. She walked up the remaining steps of her own front porch, pushed open the front door and relished, for just a moment, the warmth and safety of her own home.

* * * * *

Walking into the house, Taylre was surprised to find it empty. She expected to walk in and find the living room, kitchen and dining room filled with people, considering the number of cars parked outside. She glanced round quickly and assumed that there must be something happening over at the neighbor's house and her grandmother had given the "ok" for people to park their cars in the driveway.

She quietly removed her shoes in the front entryway and made her way toward her grandmother's bedroom. She knocked gently on the closed door. When there was no answer, Taylre opened the door slowly, its hinges squeaking slightly. The room was darkened, and Taylre was surprised to find that it was vacant. She moved back out through the door, closing it noiselessly. She turned and suddenly jumped, shocked to find a man standing in the darkened hallway, his hands folded neatly in front of himself, his mouth exhibiting a brief smile, but his eyes simply staring, showing no emotion whatsoever.

Covering her mouth to hold back the full scream that she wanted to let out, Taylre abruptly realized that the man was someone she knew, Mr. Roberts, the town's general manager. Mr. Roberts worked with Taylre's grandmother. He was considered the "number two" man in the town of Alder Cove, next to that of the Mayor.

Taylre brought her hand down from her mouth, recovering slightly from her initial fright.
"Mr. Roberts," she managed to say, her voice trembling faintly, "I'm sorry. You startled me."

"It is I that should be sorry, Taylre. I didn't mean to scare you," he said, his eyes remaining emotionless, his smile present, but not real. "I shouldn't have snuck up on you like that. I apologize."

"That's okay," Taylre responded tentatively, suddenly realizing that she had already seen Mr. Roberts tonight. His fake smile reminded her of the brief encounter in the neighbor's backyard where Terrance crouched animal-like in the bushes. She tilted her head questionably. "What are you doing here?" She asked, trying to remain respectful, but at the same time wanting to exhibit her right to curiosity. *How,* she thought, *did you get here so quickly? I just saw you in the backyard staring at Terrance.*

"Is my grandmother here? Did she let you in?" She asked.

Mr. Roberts laughed quietly, "Ask and ye shall receive. Knock, and it shall be opened unto you, " he said, his voice displaying an annoying melodious quality. "So many questions young Miss Anders, though it is always healthy to ask, just like the

Bible instructs us to do. Nevertheless, there is no need to worry. Your grandmother is here. She sent me out to make sure you were... taken care of."

"But where is she, Mr. Roberts?" Taylre asked, her courage now starting to take control.

"She's here," he said again, this time indicating with the delicate sweep of his hand that he meant the closed door he was standing in front of, the parlor.

"She's in a very important...meeting, and cannot be disturbed at the moment. You understand, don't you?" Mr. Roberts brought his hand back to clasp the other once again in front of himself.

Taylre was becoming irritated. Mr. Roberts' manner was too robotic, his smile, she could see, was fake, and there was no doubt in her mind that something iniquitous was going on in the room behind him. In fact, her intuition suggested that Mr. Roberts' job at this very moment was to keep her away at all costs. This was the most disturbing thing of all.

Taylre's relationship with her grandmother had always been extremely close, at least until recently, but this seemingly forceful blockage of her way into the room caused Taylre to shudder with concern and fear.

"Mr. Roberts," she said, standing a bit straighter, and enlivening a small amount of confidence. "This is my home. I need to go into that room and wish my grandmother a goodnight. I feel that is my right."

Again, Mr. Roberts chuckled and lifted his head and hands in the air as if he were addressing a large church congregation and began to quote more of the Bible saying: "'Then Peter opened his mouth, and said, of a truth I perceive that God is no respecter of persons!'" He slowly lowered his arms back to his sides and looked at Taylre as if she were a lowly, simple little child. "Of course, it's your right my dear. But right now your grandmother is busy and you," he said, grabbing hold of Taylre's shoulders, turning her forcefully around and pushing her in the direction of her own bedroom, "must go to bed. Your grandmother will be in when she is done; no sooner."

The strength in Mr. Roberts' hands as he seized Taylre's shoulders caused her to feel an overwhelming repugnance for the man. Yet at the same time a sudden and distinct fear that if she tried to force her way, he would hurt her. She glanced back quickly as she moved toward her room catching just a glimpse of a flickering light emanating from beneath the door to the parlor and with it some faint, ghostly whispers.

CHAPTER 8

Operation Book Salvage

The diminishing night slithered away like a deadly viper. Its black ugly head rearing itself upon the new morning in the form of a yawning creature that crouched low in the deep, dark river, unsatisfied from its evening meal. An eerie sigh escaped the beast's gaping mouth, with a putrid stench that rose and became a pale mist.

The vapor, ascending the banks of the river, stretched itself over the land, joining with the soft dews of morning and turning them toxic. The cattle that instinctually remained aloof from the edges of the river, turned and ran from the poisonous haze; a warning from somewhere deep inside their simple minds caused them to flee the unseen but detected danger.

As the mist drifted along the ground, it gathered in more of the delicate, soothing dews, turning them black and ugly. With its momentum quickening, building upon itself like an evil army forcing innocent recruits to join its ranks, it finally reached the edge of Alder Cove.

Descending into the streets and alleyways, the playgrounds and buildings, the roaming haze intruded upon its sleeping victims like a thief in the night. Children were stirred from their pleasant dreams with nightmares. Parents were roused from their slumber with calls for help and the horrified whimpers of innocent minds now infected.

A short distance across town where the mist had not entered, Devon lay asleep in his bed. In his mind, some distant memories, some flicker of vision, far beyond that of a normal dream, appeared in the form of a fisherman. His rain soaked slicker glistening in a dusky evening light; his white beard shimmering with drops of accumulated water. The man stood at the helm of a boat, leaning comfortably on the ship's wheel while he steered the boat through mountainous waves. He seemed calm as he went about his work, as if he had ridden these waves a thousand times. Suddenly, Devon found himself standing next to the man, fighting the tossing and turning of the wind and the waves. He felt the frigid drops of rain on his face and was unexpectedly chilled to the bone. He tried, in vain, to warm himself, but when he let go of the railing he found himself tossed, almost falling over the edge into the unfathomable, murky waters. But just as he felt he was going to go over the side, the comforting grip of the man pulled him to his feet, steadying him, urging him with the slight movement of his head to grab hold of the rail. When he did, the railing became Devon's source of power and strength.

Still holding on to the wheel, the man turned to Devon and spoke, his voice raised to a shout over the sound of the tumult. "You think these waters are bad? You ain't seen nothin' yet. No, lad, you ain't seen nothing yet. It gets much worse. But fear not," he said, his face displaying a contagious smile. "It'll get better soon enough, it always does. Just be sure to look for the light of the stones, lad. It's just like the rail: hold on and they'll lead you in the right direction."

Then, leaning down, looking straight into Devon's eyes he whispered sharply, "Hold the stones high, let their light shine and live!"

Devon woke with a start. He gasped inwardly, looking around the room expectantly, assuming he would see the thrashing waves and the wind-swept deck of a boat, but all was still. His room was quiet with only the soft chirping of a bird outside his window and the subtle tint of morning light seeping through the curtains.

Devon swung his legs to the floor, steadied himself, ran his fingers through his hair and breathed deeply. He walked across the cold, wooden floor; loose boards creaking as he cautiously stepped into the hallway. At once, the pungent smell of fresh paint struck his senses while he descended the stairs. His mom and dad, dressed in tattered t-shirts and old blue jeans, were rolling yellow paint onto the kitchen walls. He stood in the entry to the kitchen, his mind swirling from the acrid fumes. Devon's dad stood by the pantry, a paint smudge running the length of his forehead "Hey Devy," he said, setting the roller in a plastic paint tray. "Good to see you finally woke up. You sleep okay?"

Devon nodded, still trying to shake the cobwebs he felt in his mind.

"You look tired," his mom said. "Would you like some breakfast?" She rose from her seated position on the floor where she was dabbing paint along the edges of the floorboards. When she stood, she swept her hand around the room and looked tenderly at Devon. "Well, what do you think? The place is starting to look good, uh?"

"Yeah," he said. "Real nice."

"Did you guys have a fun time yesterday?" she said, moving to the stove where a platter full of scrambled eggs and bacon sat cooling. She scooped some of the food onto a plate and placed it into the microwave, the smells of good cooking blending with the freshly applied paint. "I noticed that both you and Zeke got some sun. Your cheeks are a bit red."

"Yeah, Taylre showed us the town. She really knows her way around." Then, from around the corner, holding a small plastic container of spackle, came Taylre, her bare knees splattered with paint and her cheeks smudged with some kind of black grease. "I think I finished filling in all of the holes in the wall in the bathroom. Is there anything else you want me to do?" Taylre asked enthusiastically.

Devon whirled around as Taylre entered, surprised, but pleased to see her. He marveled at how quickly she managed to make herself feel at home, wondering, too, why she was in their house so early.

"No, come and sit. You've done so much already. Would you like some eggs too, Taylre?" Mrs. Proper said.

"I would love some," Taylre responded, moving rapidly over to the table, giving Devon a gentle pat on his head then sitting, fork in hand ready to eat. She smiled at Devon, but eyed both Mr. and Mrs. Proper. When she decided they were occupied with other chores and not paying attention to either her or Devon, she mouthed the words: *Did you have any more dreams?* Overly exaggerating each vowel as she tried to convey her silent message.

Devon easily caught her meaning, and then he too glanced over at his parents deciding that they were indeed completely engaged in other activities. He mouthed back a simple but firm response, emphasized with the rapid nodding of his head: *yes!* The cheerful look in Taylre's eyes faded quickly at Devon's emphatic response. She took the offered plate from Mrs. Proper and began to eat, though her appetite was fading as quickly as her optimism.

A soft squeaking sound from the stairs made everyone turn to see Zeke descending from his room. His red hair was matted to one side of his head while the other side stood straight up; his face had a crease along the left cheek where his pillow had left its mark. He rubbed his eyes vigorously, seemingly unaware that he had an attentive audience watching his waking routine. When he finally noticed his watchers, he appeared indifferent. Even the sight of Taylre sitting at the kitchen table didn't affect him. He simply made his way to a chair, plopped himself into it, poured himself a large glass of orange juice, and drained its contents. When he was done, he slammed the glass down on the table, looked up and noted, with a complete lack of concern, the surprised stares from his family. "What?" he said, wiping his mouth with the back of his hand.

Zeke's mom and dad smiled to themselves and went back to their chore of painting. Taylre continued to stare, her look of concern tempered a bit by Zeke's comical morning routine. Devon stared too. However, his head shook with more of a disgusted look. "You look like such a doofus," Devon said. " Maybe you oughta' do a mirror check before you come down in the morning."

Zeke ignored Devon's poke at him. He decided it was too early in the day to deal with his little brother's attitude.

Taylre made a quick motion with her head. Zeke, noting her gesture, understood that he and Devon were to follow her outside. He looked down at his attire, but didn't care that anyone might see him outside dressed in only his pajamas. *Nobody will be out at this time of day anyway*, he thought.

Instead of exiting through the front door as Zeke had expected, Taylre led them out through the back door onto an awning-covered patio. Well used patio furniture was scattered around in no particular fashion. Apparently, Mr. Proper had not had time yet to set up the furniture in an orderly manner. The trio grabbed chairs and dragged them together keeping to the cooler, shaded areas.

As they seated themselves, Zeke noted how hot it was. The sun was barely up an hour and the temperature was already smothering. The gentle sea breezes that usually blew through town were nonexistent this morning; a heavy humidity weighed down upon them.

Zeke removed the sweatshirt he put on just before coming outside. Perspiration was already beginning to settle on his forehead. As he glanced at Devon and Taylre, he could see that they too were starting to feel the warmth.

Taylre picked up a torn piece of cardboard from an old discarded box and waved it in front of her face, desperately trying to fan away the heat. She then looked around, glancing over her shoulder toward the house and the back door. When she felt certain no one was listening she grew very serious. Her face took on an adult expression, her brow furrowed in concentration. "There is something definitely going on," she began, her words hushed, but absolute. "When I walked into my house last night, there was some sort of secret meeting going on. It was freaky."

"Meeting? what kind of a meeting?" Zeke asked, leaning in closer to hear Taylre's sharp whispers.

"I'm not sure. There were a bunch of people. I'm sure of that. They were in the parlor with the lights off, candles were lit instead," she was rushing her words now, her manner becoming anxious.

"Who were they?" Zeke said.

"I don't know," Taylre responded

"Well, what were they saying?" Zeke muttered, his voice revealing anxiety and irritation.

"I couldn't hear anything, just whispers." Taylre said, picking up on Zeke's edgy tone and eyeing him with a restrained stare.

"Was your grandma there?" Zeke asked.

"Yes, but they wouldn't let me see her, and when I got up this morning she was gone. No note, no message, nothing." Taylre was now edging toward hysteria, her voice rising with each response to Zeke's questions.

"Okay, just settle down," Zeke urged. "Let's go back to last night. You say 'they' wouldn't let you see your grandma. Who is 'they'?"

Taylre was trying hard to slow her breathing. Devon moved closer to her, patting her gently on the back, his concern evident on his worried face. "Mr. Roberts," she said, almost spitting the words out as she spoke them. "He's the 'they'. The person who wouldn't let me see grandma."

Zeke could see the glare in Taylre's eyes. It was evident she despised the man. He urged her to go on. "Who is Mr. Roberts?" he asked.

"A man who works for the Mayor," she said. "He's creepy. I've never liked him. And after last night, I like him even less, if," she emphasized, "that's even possible."

Taylre continued with her narrative, describing in detail the eerie mood that prevailed in her house the night before. Zeke sat back and pondered the events in Taylre's house as well as the one in the backyard where Terrance hunched over like a wounded animal. *Was there a connection?* he wondered.

Taylre spoke up again, "And let's not forget that Devon dreamed about the monster again," turning to Devon who sat cross legged in a weather worn chair.

He perked up at the mention of his name, looking at Taylre then at Zeke, "I had a dream, that's true, but it wasn't about the monster, not this time."

"Sorry," Taylre said. "I just assumed that when you said you had a dream that it was the same as before."

"No, not this time," Devon said, shaking his head. "This one was actually...I don't know...pleasant, but at the same time very real. It was as if I was actually there."

"Well, this sounds positive," Zeke said. "Maybe there's something to this new dream. I assume it's a new dream, right? Not something you've had before."

"It's new," Devon responded. " A new place. A completely new situation. And the man, it's as if it was someone I should know, because he certainly acted like he knew me."

"There was a man in the dream?" Taylre inquired.

"Yeah, a fisherman, I think," Devon responded.

Both Taylre and Zeke were becoming more interested by the moment. They leaned in closer, fearing that perhaps someone might overhear their conversation. Taylre looked around, making sure they were truly alone. "What did he look like?" she asked. "And what was he doing in the dream?"

Devon began to slowly relate everything he could remember. At times, he found it easier to close his eyes and visualize the scene. When he did it all came back to him vividly, as if he was, again, really there. He described the feel of the wind, the dripping cold rain, the tossing of the boat, and the gentle grip of the man as he steadied him, keeping him from falling over the side into the dark, merciless water. When he shared the part about the man speaking to him, Zeke and Taylre became even more attentive. They had Devon repeat the words the man stated several times until Devon's annoyance came to a boil. "How many more times do you want me to say it?" he said. "I've told you, all he said was to 'hold the stones high, let their light shine, and live', that's all."

Zeke mulled the words over and over in his mind. "Well, the only thing I can think of is that the Captain mentioned something about stones in the story he told us yesterday. The stones in the Captain's story glowed. Do you think they could somehow be the same?"

Devon nodded his head slowly. "I guess so. They were the ones that gave the northern people light in their boats."

"Right, glowing stones," Zeke emphasized. "Maybe there's something more about these magic stones in the Captain's big book he had. Maybe if we ask him, he'll let us look through the book for ourselves."

Taylre snorted, "Are you joking? You heard the Captain, he said all this stuff was a bunch of, what did he say? oh, yeah, fish bait. Remember? Nothin' but fish bait." she said, mimicking the Captain's pirate voice. "Do you really think he's going to let us indulge this myth by allowing us to read the book again? No way," she said emphatically.

"Well, it's worth a try, don't you think?" Zeke said, his voice expressing a harsher tone than he had intended.

"Listen," Taylre said, "You may think that you know the Captain, but you've only met him once. I've been around this place my whole life, and I can tell you, the Captain is not one to mess with. He was friendly yesterday, but that was because you were new. Trust me, you do not want to see that man when he gets mad. I have heard stories about him tearing places apart when someone got him angry. I say we just let this one go. There's got to be something else to this stones-in-the-dream thing."

"We can't give up that quickly, Taylre. If you think that the Captain won't take us to see the book, then what's to stop us from going to the boat and looking for ourselves. The Captain doesn't need to know," Zeke responded, a look of impending adventure lighting up his face like a flash from a signal flare.

"Are you crazy!" Taylre screamed. "Do you have any idea how much trouble we could get in if we got caught?"

"So we don't get caught," Zeke said easily. "It'll be simple. It's not as if we're breaking in. The Captain keeps the boat open. Nothing's locked. We just walk over there, quietly slip onto the boat, go down and open the chest. You saw that lock. It was all rusted, the Captain didn't even use a key to get it open."

Taylre was shaking her head; her hands were pressed up to her face squishing in her cheeks. "No, no, no. This is a nutty idea," she looked to Devon imploringly. "Help me out here, Devon. Talk some sense into your brother. I think he's starting to go insane."

"I don't know," Devon responded. "Maybe Zeke has a thought here, for once."

Taylre stared at Devon dumbfounded. She had hoped that at least Devon would offer her some support. "I can't believe what I'm hearing. You're both nuts."

"Think about it, Taylre," Devon continued. "I dreamed about the Korrigan, I drew a picture of it, and then we see almost the exact same thing in the book of the Captain's. Now I dream about a man, who, by the way seemed pretty real, who tells me about light, and stones, and holding things up to be safe. There's no way that all of this can be coincidence."

"But the Captain! You guys, I'm telling you, you do not want to mess with him. He has a really bad temper. I'd be terrified if he caught us in his boat looking over things he specifically said were nothing but nonsense."

"You'd be more terrified of the Captain than you would of this Korrigan thing?" Zeke asked. "Because if this thing turns out to be real, then I can tell you, we're in for a lot more trouble from *it* than we would be from the Captain.

"You admitted yourself that you think something is definitely going on around here. Those were your own words. So if it's true, if something bad *is* happening here, then we need to figure out what it is and find someone who can help get rid of it," Zeke leaned back in his tattered patio chair. He'd said all he could say to Taylre. It was up to her now to decide.

Taylre stood up and began to pace. She kept wringing her hands together; stress and worry written all over her face. Finally she sat down heavily, her breath coming out in long drawn out sighs. "Fine," she said, spitting the word out with scorn. "But we do this my way. You two follow my lead. If I say we leave then we leave. No questions, okay?"

The boys nodded, "Absolutely," Zeke said. "Whatever you say goes." Then Zeke smiled a weak but impish smile, feeling the delight of a debate well ended.

"Fair enough," Taylre said. "Now let's figure out how we're going to do this."

Zeke turned to his brother and nudged him slightly on the shoulder, "You're closest to the back door. Go inside and grab the pad of paper with the magnet on the back. The one that's stuck to the front of the refrigerator."

Devon pushed Zeke's hand off of his shoulder and scowled at him. Then he turned reluctantly and ran in the house to retrieve the pad. When he returned, Zeke took the paper from him, opened it up to a clean page and titled the top of it:

Operation Book Salvage

The three then slouched over the table like a group of army generals developing a complicated attack, and began to plot their moves.

CHAPTER 9

Storm Warning

The first thing Zeke put down on the paper was a detailed list. Zeke and Devon had only been in Alder Cove a short time, yet the catalog of strange occurrences was mounting. They all three agreed that in order to justify the rather bold expedition they were about to embark upon, they needed a good backing of information as a basis for action.

Zeke, because of his elegant handwriting, was elected chief scribe. He began by placing a neatly written "1" in the upper left hand corner of the paper, just under the bold title. Below this, he added numbers two through ten, the writing equally neat and tidy.

"We all have to think hard here," he said, looking intently at the other two conspirators. "What are some things that have occurred over the last day or so that have seemed somewhat suspicious or just down right strange?"

Devon was the first to speak up, "I think the first thing we have to mention is the Korrigan dream. It felt real, it was creepy, and let's not forget that we saw the same thing in the Captain's book."

Zeke nodded, "Good. We'll put that as number one." And then as an after thought said, "By the way, do you still have that drawing?"

Devon thought a moment, "Yeah, I do, but it's upstairs in my room. I put it in a safe place."

"Good, we'll need to hold onto that. Make sure you don't lose it. Now, what about number two?"

Taylre spoke next, "Well, there's the Terrance thing. You know, the kid sitting under the bush in that back yard. That was pretty strange, considering Terrance, at least as far as I know, has always been a pretty good kid. Plus, I can't help but feel that something weird was going on." A sudden look of recognition appeared on her face. "Did I mention that I saw Mr. Roberts in the backyard?" she said, her eyes wide with panic.

Zeke shook his head. "No, you didn't!" he said sharply, his attention turned completely on Taylre, his list temporally forgotten.

"He was there, standing back in the shadows, but he was definitely there. I didn't think there was anything to it until I saw him in my house last night. As far as I know, Mr. Roberts doesn't even live in this neighborhood, so why would he just happen to show up in the backyard last night? There's got to be a connection somehow."

Zeke pondered Taylre's words. He was beginning to also feel that there had to be some connection; something just didn't seem right. He dutifully wrote down "Terrance" for number two, and in the number three slot he wrote: Mr. Roberts - in backyard and in Taylre's house just moments after leaving backyard.

"Alright, now we're getting somewhere," he said, pencil poised to write next to the number four. "What about this 'meeting' thing last night in your house? What do you think that was all about?"

"I'm not sure," Taylre responded. "After the incident with Mr. Roberts, I went to my room, shut my door tight, and didn't come out until early this morning. I have to admit, I was pretty scared."

"Did you look around before you came over here, or did you just leave?" Zeke asked.

"I went to my grandma's room, she wasn't there, and it didn't seem like she'd been there all night. The bed was still made and didn't look like it had been slept in. When I saw that, I came right over here."

Zeke wrote: Strange meeting - grandma gone all night. He looked up from his list.
"Let's go over to your house and investigate," he said enthusiastically. "Maybe we'll pick up some clues as to what was really going on there last night."

Devon suddenly piped in, "What about the Captain's boat and the book?"

"We'll go there right after we look around Taylre's house. Besides," Zeke said, "Maybe by then the Captain will be pre-occupied with serving lunch in the café. He won't even notice us on his boat."

*   *   *   *   *

Thunderstorms have often held a powerful influence over many ancient cultures around the world. The Romans believed thunderstorms to be battles waged by Jupiter who hurled light-ening bolts forged by Vulcan. Native Americans believed them to be caused by the servants of the Great Spirit, the Thunder-birds. The Northern People, those who were the ancient inhab-itants of Alder Cove, believed that Thor, the son of Odin, using his mighty hammer Mjollnir, caused thunder and lightening to threaten the sky as he waged battle against the Frost Giants. Whatever the cause, the storm that was brewing in the sky above Alder Cove was becoming stronger by the minute. As the heat of the morning shifted to a sweltering afternoon, the warm, moist air surrounding the now cursed land rose and joined with the cooler air of the higher elevations. Cumulus clouds were rapidly developing, amassing thousands of gallons of water, cooling it, freezing it, and turning it into frozen chunks of disaster.

Devon was the first to hear the rumblings of thunder high above and to the south of the town. Rufus cowered in a corner where the house and the steps connected. His low growl echoed the thunder's drumming. Devon instinctually looked up from his position on the front steps of Taylre's house, afraid to enter with Taylre and Zeke; he felt an odd sensation upon entering the house earlier; the hair on his neck felt electrified and he felt a sudden lurch in his stomach. He decided the porch outside would be the best place to wait while Zeke and Taylre carried out their investigation.

Inside, the two sleuths crept about quietly. Zeke kept picking up knick-knacks here and there, looking at them closely and replacing them in their former position. Taylre would look over and glare at Zeke, her stare asking an unvoiced question, *why are you picking that up? It has nothing to do with what we're looking for.* Zeke ignored her glares, his curiosity in the strange surroundings overshadowing his fear of Taylre's reprisals.

They moved down the hallway, its wide pathway accentuated by ornate crown molding and a floor covered in smooth, shiny hard wood. The atmosphere seemed unwelcoming to Zeke. There was a heaviness in the stale air of the house that reminded him of a scene from the horror movie *The Shining* and Zeke expected to see, in a macabre, distorted way, a pair of pale-skinned twin sisters standing hand in hand at the end of the hallway.

As they approached the closed door to the parlor, Taylre reached out to turn the glass knob. She stopped abruptly, her hands trembling slightly. Then she swung around slowly, her head cocked a little to one side and stared at Zeke in a most curious manner. He approached her tentatively. "What's the matter?" he whispered.

Taylre widened her eyes and shook her head violently. She pointed toward the door mouthing the words, "*I think there's someone in there!*"

Zeke felt a shiver rise up his spine; his scalp tingled. They both leaned in closer, placing their ears gently up against the door, listening intently.

There was a barely audible fluttering with an occasional click-ing sound originating from behind the door. Zeke tried to form an image in his mind of what the sound could be. He thought it was familiar, perhaps someone shuffling around the room, but he didn't think so. It was something else, something he'd heard before. He changed positions with Taylre and took hold of the glass door knob, its jagged edges cool to the touch. Slowly, he turned the knob and inched the door open. When he'd opened the door just a few inches, he slipped his head through, his body tense and ready to flee at the slightest noise or movement. All at once, he was struck with the pungent, smoky scent of incense.

The room was dimly lit. The curtains had been drawn. As Zeke's eyes adjusted to the light, he could see that the room was vacant. The fluttering sound was nothing but an oscillat-ing fan that sat in the corner, and it clicked each time it swung to the left. Zeke pushed the door open, giving Taylre the "ok" sign to come in. As they moved a short pace into the room they did so apprehensively, there was a heaviness in the air, a dark-ness that repelled them both. They stood for a long time in the doorway, their desire to enter any further discouraged by the ominous feeling in the room.

As Zeke surveyed the parlor, he could see that it was simply furnished. Dark hardwood covered the floor with a faded throw rug placed in the center. A fireplace sat in the corner, its mantle covered lightly with small framed pictures, candle sticks, and a matching set of model sailing ships, their sails open to some unfelt wind. The fireplace was clean. The grate was still shiny, as if it had never been used. The walls of the room were mostly bare, except for the occasional framed picture showing fishing boats on the sea, their nets being hauled from the water laden with fish.

The throw rug had four unlit candles in the center, which were positioned in a square with a burning incense stick sitting in a richly carved wooden tray in the middle; a sliver of gray smoke drifted up then dissipated throughout the room as the push of air from the fan encountered the smoke. Surrounding the candles was a circle of chairs that eerily faced each other.

Zeke became brave and walked farther into the room; Taylre remained in the doorway as the comfort of the well-lit hallway steadied her. He ventured toward the circle of chairs, gently sliding one of them to the side and entered the circle. All at once he was struck with blackness, almost like a heavy, wet curtain had been draped over his face. He felt as if he were suffocating. He tried to push away the unseen cover that enveloped his face, but nothing was there. His throat tightened and his lungs began to burn. His eyes widened with terror; he was sure that he was about to die. His knees gave way and he fell to the floor heavily, his head brushing the side of one of the unlit candles and knocking it over. Then, just as quickly as the blackness invaded his mind, it left. Zeke found he could now breathe, the air entered his nostrils like a cool breeze in the evening.

Taylre rushed over to the now scattered circle of chairs, her fear of entering the room overcome with the sight of Zeke struggling with some unseen assailant. She grabbed hold of Zeke's leg and pulled, dragging him out of the circle, off of the throw rug, and onto the smoothness of the hardwood floor.

When she had Zeke out of the room and into the hallway, Taylre knelt beside him, trying to lift him into a sitting position. Zeke coughed a few times as he sat up, his breathing coming easier, the paleness fading from his face.

"What just happened?" Zeke said, struggling to stand up.

Taylre took his arm and tried to steady him as he stood, "We've got to leave, Zeke," Taylre said sharply.

Zeke turned to her. The look in her eyes convinced him to go, no questions.

Taylre grabbed hold of Zeke's arm and yanked him down the hallway, past the kitchen and outside through the back door since it was closer than the front. With Zeke still in tow, Taylre led him around to the front where Devon still sat on the front porch. Rufus rose up quickly from his slumbering position on a shaded part of the lawn. Startled from his nap, he appeared to take on a defensive manner until he finally recognized Zeke and Taylre. He then began to eagerly wag his tail, a sheepish grin actually appearing on his face.

Devon also looked up from his daydream, a bit shocked at the sudden appearance of Zeke and Taylre; he stepped down to meet them. Instantly he could see something was wrong. Zeke, still a bit colorless from his evil encounter, had a dazed look. Taylre had a look of fear, mingled with determination.

"Let's go back to your house," she said, not stopping for a response.

"Wait, wait a minute," Zeke said, rushing toward her and grabbing her arm. "Let's just catch our breath, relax, and think for a moment. We don't need to rush off to my house. There's no answers there."

Taylre turned, frustrated, " I'm not going back in that house," she said. "We've got to go back to your house and tell your mom and dad what's going on. Something's happening here that's beyond our control or comprehension. I'm scared, too, that something bad has happened to my grandma. I'm sure of it." Tears began to form in her already red and swollen eyes.

"Taylre," Zeke said, " What are we going to tell my mom and dad? That there's a monster around somewhere? That we know this because Devon had a dream and we read about it in a book? They're not going to believe us. They'll think were goofing around."

"But what about my grandma? Where is she?" she said, sobbing lightly.

"I don't know, Taylre. Maybe she went to work early. Maybe she didn't want to wake you too early, but let's not jump to any conclusions here. We've got to figure this thing out before we go to any adults. We've got to have some proof that something's really happening. Right now we have nothing."

"I'm not so sure about that," she said, lowering her head and shaking it. "What I saw in that room is proof enough for me that something *is* going on. There's no question."

Zeke shuddered at the mention of the parlor. He knew there was something going on too, but how could he explain it to his mom and dad without them thinking he was crazy. "Taylre," he said. "What happened back there in the parlor? Did you see something?"

For a moment there was only a confused silence between the group. Even Rufus could sense the tension that was building.

They shuffled over to the opposite side of the road. Rufus tagged along, his tongue hanging out of his mouth, panting from the heat. They seated themselves on the edge of the warm curb. Taylre took off her glasses, rubbing her swollen cheeks then holding her hands over her eyes as if to block out a memory, but at the same time hoping to release its hold upon her.

"When you pushed aside the chair and entered the circle," she began, trembling slightly, "something black dropped from the ceiling. It didn't have any distinct features, but it looked like a person, only smoky and misty-like. And when it dropped, it landed on your shoulders, like it was sitting on them. As soon as it landed on you I could see you start to struggle, like you couldn't catch your breath. You kept waving your arms around, and I thought you were going to push the thing off your shoulders, but when you waved your hands they went right through the smoky figure - as if it weren't even there. Then you fell. I wanted to run to you and help, but, I'm sorry, I was so scared." She began to weep softly. In a few moments she regained her composure.

"When you fell," she continued, "your head hit one of the candles and knocked it over. As soon as that happened, the black thing rose up off your shoulders and went up into the ceiling where it came from. It's as if you somehow broke through a barrier when you knocked down the candle causing a spell to be broken."

As Taylre related the events that took place inside the house, Devon sat listening, his eyes wide, his body leaning into catch every word. "Do you remember any of this, Zeke?" Devon asked.

"I remember all of it," Zeke responded. "The only thing I didn't know was that the blackness I *felt* could also be seen."

"So what was going on in that room last night?" Devon asked.

"I can't tell *what* was going on, but I can tell you it *wasn't* just an ordinary meeting," Taylre said.

"Definitely not," Zeke agreed. "I think now, more than ever, we need to look in that book of the Captain's and see if we can find out what's going on. That book is where we're going to find some answers. I'm certain of it. Devon's latest dream may be the clue we're looking for."

Devon sat scratching his head, mulling over what Zeke was saying about the book. "I hope so," Devon replied apprehensively. "But I'm not sure. Something just doesn't seem right."

"I know," Zeke responded. "But I think we're all a little spooked by what just happened. I say we keep with the plan: head over to the Captain's boat, find the book, and hopefully start putting pieces together to make some sense of things." Devon and Taylre nodded their heads reluctantly.

"Alright," Taylre finally said. "We'll go. But remember, if I say we leave, then we leave."

Rufus was the first to stand, as if he knew from the way his companions spoke that the day still held more walking, barking and sniffing. Sadly, though, Devon grabbed hold of his collar and lugged him unwillingly back to the Proper's yard. Devon tied Rufus securely to a lengthy rope that connected to a well worn and weathered dog house. As Devon shuffled away, Rufus circled three times in the shade of the house, laid down in the drying grass and watched solemnly as the three adventurers made their way toward the main part of town and the piers. As they passed Taylre's house, however, they kept to the opposite side of the street, fearing the darkness that lay hidden there, feeling as if something sinister and dark were watching them as they walked by.

CHAPTER 10

Rusted Locks

The problem, as far as Zeke could see, was that the angles were all wrong. If they tried to approach from the north, the Captain would see them from the counter through the large paned window of his café, Typhoon Jacks. If they approached from the south, then the Captain would be able to see them through the reflection in the big mirror that hung on the wall opposite the lunch counter. Zeke considered that the possibility of the Captain noticing them sneaking up from the south and spotting them in the mirror would be remote, at best, but he was not about to take any chances. Besides, Taylre would not risk the possibility of being seen in either direction. They simply had to find another way to get around back and to the boat without being seen. Creeping in through the Captain's café and through his back door just wasn't a viable plan.

As the three cousins stood concealed in the doorway of an antique furniture shop, underneath the shade of an awning, Devon considered the options. "What if we entered through the gate at the marina?" Devon suggested.

"We can't," responded Taylre. "The gate's always locked. The only people that can get through it are those who own boats and have a key. The pier is considered private property."

"But the Captain was able to get to his boat by walking out his back door," said Zeke.

"Right," Taylre agreed, "but that's because he has a business on the pier owner's property. Everybody who runs a business on the sea-side has access to the pier. I guess you could say it's one of the perks of having a shop on that side."

"So you're saying that all of the businesses have a back door like the Captain's, and they can walk out into the marina anytime they want?" Zeke asked.

"As far as I know," said Taylre, shrugging her shoulders.

"Then why aren't we considering one of the other shops to cut through? Surely one of them will let us through," Zeke suggested.

"Maybe we could just swim around," added Devon sheepishly.

"Yeah, right," said Zeke. "And while we're at it, why don't we build a helicopter and fly over the top," he said sarcastically.

"Hey, I'm just trying to help, dork."

"Who're you callin' a dork, jerk."

"*I'm* callin' you a dork, monkey face."

"Alright, knock it off you two," Taylre reprimanded, forcefully stepping between the two combatants. "We don't have time for bickering and arguing. If we're going to get to the Captain's boat, we've got to work together."

Zeke and Devon glared at each other momentarily. Devon finally smiled his cheesy grin and lightly punched Zeke in the arm. Zeke smiled back, shaking his head.

"Jerk."

"Dork."

Taylre watched the exchange briefly, then she too shook her head. "Boys," she mumbled.

Taylre turned her attention back to the task at hand. She looked up and down the sea-side shops and considered which one would be the best to go through. Suddenly, her eyes rested on a particular store:

Zelda's Used Books

"Perfect," she said, more to herself than to the boys.

"What's perfect?" Zeke said.

"The book shop. That's how we'll get in."

She moved quickly down the street, the brothers trailing behind, always aware of *Typhoon Jacks* across the street.

"Don't look at the café," she said, keeping her head low as she walked. "We don't want to appear conspicuous." The boys followed suit by looking through shop windows or peering up at the sky, pretending they were completely engaged in things other than trying to sneak into the marina. However, the fact of the matter was that their attempt at being unnoticeable made them even more prominent. Anyone who might have been watching them would have known that they were definitely up to something. A fact that the Captain recognized immediately, as he sat in the barren café, watching the three investigators walk past.

* * * * *

Zelda's Book Store was established in Alder Cove in 1965. The original owner, Zelda, died ten years ago. Her daughter, Karen, was the new owner of the store and she tried her best to keep the shop the way her mother kept it: hospitable, welcoming and full of the best books that money could buy.

Solid, dark wood shelves lined the walls, and each shelf was jammed with hardbacks and paperbacks. The rich smell of leather combined with the musty scent of yellowed pages permeated the shop. One section of the store was reserved for children's books. There sat a rocking chair on top of a colorful Mother Goose throw rug. On Tuesday and Thursday afternoons, Karen would sit in the old chair and read fairytales, fables and stories of adventure; young audiences would become enraptured as Karen read from the leather bound books, changing voices to suit the characters while waving her arms in mock sword fighting, bowing her head in gallant poses and performing pretend embraces in happy-ever-after endings.

This Tuesday afternoon, however, brought no young visitors into the shop to hear the stories Karen had set aside to read. The floor near the ornately carved rocking chair remained empty. Only the stifling heat of the day filled the vacant shop. Grudgingly, Karen was becoming accustomed to the lack of customers.

As she relaxed in a handsome leather chair behind the short counter, sipping iced green tea from a crystal goblet her mother used to use, she was surprised, but pleased to see three young people walk into her store.

The girl who entered first, looked familiar to Karen. Her tall, lanky figure was hard to forget. The two boys who followed were obviously brothers; their reddish blond hair and freckled faces made them look almost identical. The only difference was that one was taller than the other.

"May I help you?" Karen said, rising slowly from her chair, its worn springs squeaking slightly as she rose. She set aside her volume of *Wuthering Heights* and placed her drink on a worn coaster atop a stack of papers on the counter.

"We're just looking," Taylre responded, eyeing the room intently, her mind seeking the best source of distraction.

"Take all the time you need," Karen said. "I'll be right here reading if you need me."

Taylre glanced quickly at Zeke and motioned with a quick nod of her head toward the back of the shop where a door stood, its faded wood façade blocked partially with empty cardboard boxes. Zeke began to move nonchalantly toward the exit to the marina. Devon mirrored Zeke's moves and tried to keep his head down, fearing his eyes would somehow give away the trio's plot.

Taylre began looking intently at some colorful travel books that were scattered on a small table. She picked one up and pretended to be interested in its contents, at the same time catching a glimpse of the full goblet of chilled tea awkwardly placed on a small stack of papers. Suddenly the idea came to her and she gently replaced the travel book and approached the shop keeper. In the mean time, Zeke and Devon continued to inch closer to the door, hoping Taylre's distraction plan would be successful.

Taylre cleared her throat. "Excuse me, Zelda is it?" Taylre said, looking quickly from the ice filled glass to Karen.

Karen looked up just as she was about to sit down. "I'm Karen, honey," she said, smiling. "Zelda was my mother, but she's passed on now."

"Oh, I'm so sorry to hear that, Karen." Taylre said, feeling truly sorry for the loss of Karen's mother since Taylre had a genuine soft spot for those who'd lost parents. "I'm wondering, would you know where I might find a hard back copy of *Twilight*?" she asked, feeling her palms unexpectedly becoming sweaty. "It's very popular right now with all of my girlfriends; I just want to keep up on the latest book."

"*Twilight*, honey. Oh, gosh, that book has been going like hotcakes. It's one of the books that seems to be keeping me in business," Karen muttered as she rose again from her leather chair. " Nothing like a good vampire love story to keep you interested."

She moved from behind the counter and strolled over to the fiction section located near the back of the shop. As she shuffled along she continued to speak. "It's awfully good to see you young people taking an interest in reading again. It seems to me young people today get too caught up in T.V. and video games to take any time out to read these days." Karen said.

As Karen rummaged around in the shelves, Taylre shifted stealthily toward the counter. She turned to look at the two boys, took a deep breath, and gave them the 'ok' sign.

Zeke moved quickly the to the door and began shifting the empty boxes out of the way. Devon acted as the lookout while Karen stood on top of a short ladder and fumbled with books high on a shelf.

While Karen remained preoccupied, Taylre inched her way toward to Karen's cup holding the cooled tea. With shaking hands, she reached down and grasped the rim of the glass with her thumb and forefinger, feeling for just a moment the slippery condensation which had formed along the edge of the goblet. Then, almost without a thought, Taylre lifted the glass upward and tipped it to the side, the contents spilling haphazardly in all directions; the papers becoming soaked and smudged. Taylre let out a muffled scream that quickly caught the attention of Karen.

With an anger creased brow, Karen stepped down swiftly from the step ladder. "Oh, now look what you've done!" she exclaimed, rushing toward the spill and trying frantically to remove soggy papers from further damage. As she focused on the mess, she paid no attention to the two boys who continued to clear a path to the door.

"I am so sorry," Taylre said, glancing at the anxious lady in front of her and shifting her gaze to the progress the boys were making at the door. Taylre made a twirling motion with her hand, urging the boys to hurry; panic was beginning to rise in her.

"Well, I can see that this isn't working," Karen said, her frustration mounting. She glared sharply at Taylre, then abandoned her attempt of mopping up the mess and turned toward a small backroom where she disappeared to find better cleaning supplies.

Taylre felt a pang of guilt. She was normally not the type to cause problems, but this, she felt, was a noble cause. Taylre ran over to the boys who were moving the last of the boxes from the door. She watched nervously as they slid it off to the side. For Taylre, the moment had arrived. Her nerves were frazzled and she couldn't wait to escape the confines of the bookstore. She reached for the door knob and turned — it was locked.

Taylre's eyes became wide with frustration and panic. Her first thought was to call it off; to tell the boys to run out the front door and forget the whole thing. But she couldn't. Something compelled her to go on.

She steadied herself and looked about the room until her eyes rested on a set of keys that were placed on the counter, a small stream of spilled tea inching its way toward them. She moved rapidly to the desk and grabbed the keys. Inside the backroom, behind a heavy curtain, Taylre could hear Karen's movements as she continued to rummage for towels.

Taylre raced back to the door, her hands shaking uncontrollably. She fumbled with the keys and attempted to insert one of them into the lock, but her trembling hands wouldn't allow it. Zeke finally took the keys from her dancing hands and confidently inserted one of them into the lock and turned...nothing happened.

He tried another, but it too had no effect. He glanced at Taylre who was waving her hands in front of her and jumping up and down as if she were about to explode, her eyes continually looking at the heavy curtain where Karen rummaged for supplies. Devon stood to the side, his arms crossed over his chest, watching the proceedings like a casual observer, a weak but amused smile smeared across his face.

Finally, Zeke inserted the last key. He turned it hopefully; eyes closed in anticipation, and opened the door. Hastily, the three slipped through the opening, closed the door quietly behind them and bolted toward the pier. The Captain's dilapidated boat was waiting a short distance away, resting in its watery hovel like an ancient bearded sage, its message of wisdom waiting to be distributed.

Karen appeared from behind the heavy curtain. She sighed and stared at the mess that remained on the counter. Then she looked up. The shop was empty. "Those gosh darn kids," she said. "It'd be better if they just stayed at home and played their video games." She continued her cleanup of the counter, oblivious to the empty boxes that lay strewn about on the floor, or the mislaid keys that dangled in the lock.

* * * * *

The Captain's boat rocked gently on soothing ripples of water. Occasionally, it would knock up against the wooden dock, but inflated, white rubber shocks that hung over the side of the boat protected its hull from damage and the dock from splintering. Seagulls were perched on the upper deck and bemoaning a cacophony of sound, like children arguing on a playground. The birds' squawking seemed to exude a kind of discomfort for the heat that continued to encompass the town; indeed, it seemed to be getting worse as the day drew on.

As the children neared the boat, a kind of relief swept over them. The ordeal at Zelda's had taken its toll. Taylre's legs still shook and Zeke was constantly looking over his shoulder, expecting to see the book lady come chasing over the wooden docks after them. Reaching the side of the boat was a welcome release of stress and worry for both of them. As far as Devon was concerned, things were going as well as could be expected. His thoughts were centered on the book and the secrets that lay hidden behind a rusted lock.

As they came to the side of the boat, each in turn slipped easily over the bulwark and on to the deck. Zeke moved quickly to the small cabin door which led down to the bottom of the boat, and tested its lock - *it* opened without difficulty.

"Taylre," Zeke said, standing with one foot on the deck and the other balanced on the first of several steep steps. "We'll need you to stand guard. If anyone approaches whistle, or shout, or stamp your foot, whatever, just do something to get our attention so we don't get caught."

"Fine," Taylre agreed, " just be quick about it. I'm nervous enough as it is."

Zeke made another step, when he stopped and looked again at Taylre. "Wait," he said, a puzzled look coming over his face.

"Am I supposed to take the book, or just look in it for information?"

Taylre shrugged her shoulders. "I don't know." Then, as if by some silent agreement, both Taylre and Zeke turned to Devon.

"What are you guys looking at me for?" Devon said.

Neither Zeke nor Taylre knew exactly why they were looking at Devon. To them it seemed that for some reason he would know the answer to the enquiry. They continued to stare, hoping their silence would press an answer.

Finally, realizing his two conspirators would not relent, Devon furrowed his brow slightly and pursed his lips in thought. "Take it, I guess. It'll give us more time to look it over."

"Okay, sounds good to me. You okay with that Taylre?" Zeke asked.

"I suppose. Let's just get moving, whatever we decide to do. I feel like we're sitting ducks out here."

Zeke and Devon proceeded down the steps, the steep grade making them both feel a little dizzy. As they reached the bottom step, Zeke looked up to see the aged trunk sitting in a tight, musty corner; the rusted lock fastened to the front. He approached the trunk hesitantly, as if it were a sacred relic requiring his reverence. He gingerly touched the lock, half expecting it to crumble off in his hands. Finally, after a few moments of gathering his nerve, he grabbed hold of the lock forcefully and tugged at it like the Captain had done previously, but nothing happened. He pulled harder, putting all of his weight into it, but still it remained unmoved. Next, he used his foot to kick at it. At first just with the tip of his shoe, but when that didn't work, he began whacking at it with his heel, but still, the lock remained firm. Taylre poked her head into the small doorway and peered down at the two brothers who were now both taking turns banging at it with their feet and any other small objects they could find.

"What's taking so long?" She hissed.

"It won't budge," Zeke shouted back, his frustration rising with each wallop. "Is there anything up there that we can use to get this open?"

Taylre looked about the deck quickly spotting a aged crowbar wedged between some rotted slats running perpendicular to the deck of the boat. She ran over and grabbed the bar, tucking it under her arm and leaping down the steep steps, her athleticism continuing to impress both Zeke and Devon. She placed it in Zeke's hands. He hefted it, feeling its solid weight, and began banging it down forcefully on the lock, but with no success.

"Here, let me try," Taylre said, grabbing the bar and swinging it across the face of the lock, managing only to chip some of the rust from its surface. Sweat was beginning to form on her forehead when suddenly a squeak sounded above them. All three lost their focus on the rusted lock and turned, looking upward, toward the direction of the sound.

The light coming in from the open door at the top of the stairs was blocked by a large silhouetted figure. Its abrupt appearance loomed before the three delinquents like a dark specter from some insane nightmare.

"You'll not be finding anything' in there that'll help ya," the voice from the open door said. "If it's answers you're lookin for, you've come to the wrong place."

CHAPTER 11

The Yarn Part II

The Captain carried his heavy bulk down the stairs, taking each step deliberately. His piercing, ominous glare penetrated the dim light that pervaded the belly of the boat. As he descended, his gaze never left the faces of the three intruders as they each stood frozen in shocked amazement and nervous trepidation. They were sure the infamous anger of the Captain would now be thrust upon them, and they would not survive the blow. When the Captain finally reached the bottom step, he inhaled deeply, letting the air move in slowly and then exhaled sharply through his slightly parted lips. He brought up his hand toward Taylre, and she involuntarily flinched.

"Give me the crowbar," he said, holding out his hand.

Taylre turned her gaze a little toward Zeke and Devon, her head remaining perfectly still. Zeke shook his head, almost imperceptibly, but Taylre noted the movement. "I...I can hold it," she said, her voice trembling faintly.

"It's not a request, Taylre," the Captain said, his voice even and emotionless. "Give me the crowbar, now," he repeated.

Taylre reluctantly held out the heavy metal bar, placing it slowly in the Captain's hand. The Captain grabbed hold of it and in one quick motion tossed it aside, its metal clanging loudly against a small table in another corner of the galley. "Sit!" he ordered.

Zeke, Devon and Taylre all looked at one another, the confusion evident in their stares. "I said sit!" the Captain bellowed.

This time all three obeyed quickly, each taking a seat on the nearest chair, fear showing in their every movement. The Captain reached back and pulled a short wooden stool in close. He sat heavily, grunting as he did, his knees creaking and cracking as he bent. He continued to stare at the youth, his face slowly changing its expression from anger to sadness. He bowed his head trying to gather his thoughts. When he finally raised his head, he had the look of a defeated man, as if he had just been received death sentence and his final moments were at hand.

"I want to apologize to the three of you," he said weakly, his voice faint and the pirate accent slightly diminished. "I have done a great disservice to ya. I lied. That's what I did. I lied. But I thought I was doin' you a favor. The problem is that I didn't expect ya to be so curious; so smart; so intelligent. I shoulda' known better. Please forgive me."

The trio simply stared, too dumbfounded to say anything. They expected to be yelled at, to be told they were thieves and crooks. They expected to be taken home to their parents and in shame have to explain what they were doing on the Captain's boat; explain how they had tricked the book lady and probably ruined her countertop. Instead, they sat in silence listening to the Captain apologize to them.

"Why?" Taylre finally managed to say. "Why are you apologizing to us when we should be saying sorry to you?"

"Because I lied," the Captain said humbly. "I lied about the Korrigan. I lied about the fact that nothing' was goin' on here in Alder Cove. I tossed aside the dream that Devon had, hopin' it was just a fluke. I was tryin' to protect ya. Ya have to believe that. But now I can see that ya know. You've obviously seen something', otherwise why would ya be here?"

"You're right," Zeke said. "We have seen some things. We're scared and we just want to find some answers. That's why we're here...to find answers...in the book."

"What makes ya think that you're going to find answers in that book?" the Captain said, indicating the trunk sitting behind them.

"Because of my other dream," Devon piped in. "I had another dream, one that seemed almost too real. But this time it wasn't about the Korrigan. This time it was a man on a boat. A kind man who told me that if we 'held the stones high we'd live'...or something like that."

"A man?" the Captain questioned, his interest suddenly piqued, causing him to sit up a little straighter in his seat. "What man? What did he look like?"

"He was old, but not too old," Devon began. "He had a dark, short beard. His eyes were green. I remember them because when he looked at me they seemed to glow...but in a nice way. He was steering an old boat and we were on the ocean. The wind was blowing and the waves were really high. At one point I thought I was going to fall over the edge, but he reached out and saved me; pulled me upright and told me to hold onto the rail, that if I did, it would steady me and help me get to where I was going. Then he leaned over and told me to...what did he say again?" Devon looked to Zeke for help.

"He said to 'hold the stones high and live,'" Zeke said. " At least that's what Devon told us: 'hold the stones high and live'. And that's why we're here. There's got to be more in the book about stones or rocks. Something that will give us more clues. We've got to read further into the book and find out exactly what's going on and how it can be stopped." Zeke leaned back in his chair, relieved to have said what he felt needed to be said.

The Captain chuckled faintly under his breath. He looked at the three sadly. "It's not there. Believe me it's not there. I've read it. I've studied it until my eyes became so blurry I couldn't make out another word. There's nothing there that will help."

"But what about the dream?" Devon asked. "If the Korrigan dream was real, then this one probably was too. So what the man said about stones must be true. It's got to be in that book."

"Not necessarily," the Captain stated. "Not if there were..." And suddenly the Captain's eyes became wide with a sudden understanding. "Another book."

"What do you mean 'another book'?" Taylre asked, leaning in closer, a determined expression showing on her face. When Zeke saw this, he felt a surge of enthusiasm; the old Taylre was back.

"What I mean," the Captain explained, his own fervor taking flight, "is that there has to be another book somewhere. A book that is the opposite of this one." Again indicating the book in the chest.

"The book in the trunk is the evil one," the Captain spat. "It has all o' the dark stories about the Korrigan and how to conjure it. It tells the stories o' the people who came over here and initially brought that filthy beast to this land. It doesn't tell how to get rid of it though...if that's possible."

"If there's another book," Zeke asked, "then where is it? *If* it even exists."

"Aye, lad," the Captain said, his pirate voice regaining its familiar intensity. "That'd be the million dollar question. Nobody that I know knows anything about another book, or where the book would lie. If we could solve that mystery, then we might be able to save this town from further visits from the Korrigan."

The Captain shifted uncomfortably on the short stool. He reached up and rubbed briskly at the rough stubble on his face as he tried, once again, to gather his thoughts, making sure that each word he spoke was accurate and direct. "Listen," he said, leaning in closely as if some unwanted listener might be nearby. "The story that I told ya about the ancient group of people who left their land and drifted over the ocean in those strangely made sailin' dishes was true. That's all written in the book. They were the first ones to conjure up the Korrigan. The book there tells exactly how to do it and the kind of evil ceremony that has to be run in order to bring it here, but now I'm beginin' to believe that there may be some parts that are missin', or possibly written another book. What I didn't tell ya was that after a few hundred years, the Korrigan quit comin' for some reason...no one knows why...it just stopped coming. Everythin' went back to normal. People were happy. They raised their families and crops in peace for many years. But then somethin happened," the Captain said, turning his gaze directly at Zeke, the pupils of his eyes contracting slightly. "And it all started, I'm sorry to say, with the Proper family. It was *your* ancestors who brought back the Korrigan."

"What?!" Zeke exclaimed incredulously. "Are you crazy? Our family wouldn't do that."

Zeke stood up abruptly and began marching toward the steps. He was offended and his pride was hurt. The Captain stood too, blocking Zeke's way and gently grabbing him by the shoulders. "Sit, young lad. I didn't mean to upset ya. If ya just give me a moment, I'll explain everything, at least as much as I know. Then, if ya still feel angry, you can leave, but not until I've said my peace - you owe me that much."

Zeke weighed the Captain's words, realizing he did owe the Captain something, considering they had just broken into his boat and tried in vain to whack the lock off of some of the Captain's personal property. He retreated reluctantly to his former seat and sat down heavily, crossing his arms and releasing a slight 'umph'. "Go ahead," he said snidely, "we're listening."

The Captain cleared his throat, reached into his vest pocket and removed his pipe and a small pouch of tobacco. He began filling the pipe slowly and methodically, his mind working over the details of what he might say, making sure that no details were left out.

Taylre looked over at the two brothers. She rolled her eyes, then mouthed the words, *This is going to be a long story*. She knew from experience that when the Captain began filling his pipe, he was preparing himself for another long yarn.

The Captain struck a match on the bottom of the stool he sat on, placing the flame to the bowl of his pipe and inhaling deeply, the sweet smoke drifting from the corners of his mouth and through his nostrils. He then leaned forward, removing the pipe as if to speak when the already dim light in the cabin grew fainter and an all-encompassing coolness entered the room. The Captain stood as if suddenly alarmed. He climbed clumsily, but efficiently, to the top of the stairs, stepping out onto the deck and staring up into the darkening sky. The three that remained below also stood, their confused expressions mirrored in each other's gaze, their minds troubled by the Captain's sudden departure. They climbed the stairs briskly, stepping out onto the deck behind the Captain. They followed his gaze and stared into the sky noting with unease a swirling mass of dark purple clouds that hung over them. The temperature had also changed drastically. One moment it was so hot that even the insects wouldn't fly, now, there existed a cool humidity that held a tangible weight. Zeke could actually see his breath as he exhaled sharply, his breathing coming in heavy, short bursts from the exerted effort of climbing the steep stairway.

"This is goin' to be bad," the Captain groaned. "We need to get below quickly. Hurry now, thar isn't much time!" he waved his arms around as if he were herding sheep into a corral, urging the three back down the steep stairs, closing the cabin door tightly behind him.

"What's happening, Captain?" Taylre asked, feeling the boat suddenly shift and sway as the wind outside picked up and the waves in the small harbor began to rise.

"A storm is a brewin' lass. A great storm the likes I've never seen. So grab a hold of somethin' and get ready to be tossed around a bit."

Suddenly, a great light flashed and a crack of thunder pierced the air. Taylre wrapped her arms around her head and screamed while Zeke and Devon fell to their knees with fright, their eyes drawn to the ceiling, expecting it to come crashing down upon their heads.

At first there was just a light patter on the deck above. Then the it became louder and heavier. Large, splashing clatter could be heard in the water around them, and a sound like breaking glass could be heard from heavy objects falling on the wooden dock. Again, the insides of the ship reverberated as another crack of thunder shook the very air itself. Zeke moved tentatively toward a small porthole, its rounded glass framed by a tight shiny metal brace. As he peered through he could see the water in the marina being agitated by wind and what appeared to be errant golf balls, launched from some unseen golf course, each sphere perfectly round and white. "Come quickly!" he called. The small group moved quickly and surrounded Zeke. They huddled around the tiny window trying to peer through the fogging lens.

The Captain grunted. "That is by far the largest hail I've ever seen," he exclaimed.

"Hail!" shouted Taylre, trying to reach her voice over the clamor of smashing ice. "How could we be having hail? Just a few moments ago, we were sweltering from the heat. Now I can almost see my breath. What in the world is going on here?"

"It's nothin from this world, I can tell ya that much lass. No, it's nothin from this world," the Captain said.

Slowly, the loud clatter from the falling chunks of ice turned to an occasional pattering. Then, only the sporadic tapping. Finally it stopped. The dark cloud that sent the destructive force drifted away and dissipated into nothingness over the ocean, as lightening flashed faintly in the distance like dying fireflies.

Slowly, the four crept up the stairs, the Captain in the lead opening the door cautiously, as if he were in a war zone, the threat of gunfire foremost in his mind. The small door opened gradually, its creaking hinges causing a nervous flutter to whisper up the spines of the three adventurers. The Captain was first to step onto the deck. He squinted as he tried to look through a fine mist that had settled on the marina. Around him, he could see the destruction of the momentary chaos: Boats had their windows shattered, pieces of the dock had been destroyed, and dead birds lay scattered on the pier; some floated on the water. A deathly stillness weighed upon the scene.

"This is a warnin'," the Captain said. "She's hungry, an when she gets hungry, she gets mad." His three companions were looking at him in stunned silence, their mouths open in wonder at what he had just said. "I guess I have some explainin' to do, don't I?" Still they stared at him, no one saying a word. "Yeah, I guess I do," he said to himself. The Captain made his way to the side of the boat where he began to untie lines that were connected to small pilings on the dock and bring aboard the white inflated fenders that hung over the side. As he worked, the Captain looked up at the shifting sky. Darkened, ominous clouds turned almost magically to white wisps of pure cotton, then to clear blue nothingness. The cold left too, just as suddenly, and the temperature jumped radically forty or fifty degrees in a single bound. He shook his head in wonder, realizing, in all his years at sea, he had never witnessed such a thing.

When the boat was free from its moorings, the Captain climbed a series of small steps that took him to the bridge. With deft hands, he turned a key and the ancient diesel engine at the back of the vessel roared to life, a puff of black smoke coughing from a smoke stack near the stern. Gingerly, the Captain shifted the throttle slowly forward and guided the boat out of the marina and into open water.

Zeke, Devon and Taylre climbed up to the bridge. Zeke leaned himself up against the window on the right hand of the Captain, while Devon and Taylre took their places directly behind and to the left. In silence the four puttered out to sea, the Captain always looking straight ahead, puffing his pipe; the three explorers used the lull to contemplate the strange occurrences that were increasing.

Finally, the Captain cleared his throat and the three looked up expectantly, their questions ready to explode from their mouths. The Captain held up his hands, like a fighter trying to block the blows of his opponent. "Now, before any of ya says anythin, because I know ya have a million questions that you're just dyin' to ask, you've got to let me speak; let me say my peace, then, once I'm done, ya can ask any question ya like. Just remember, I may not have all the answers you're lookin for. There's still a lot of questions I have too. But maybe, if we put our heads together, we can sort this whole thing out and come up with a solution. Agreed?" The three nodded, afraid that if they did speak the questions would come pouring out like the rain and hail that had just assaulted the town.

"Good," the Captain said, trying to smile, but making it look more like a painful grimace. "I'll start from as far back as I know, what with the studying I've done in the book and all, and I'll add to it the things I know outside of the book, after that, ask me anything ya like," he said this with a hesitant sigh as his hands trembled and his tightening grip on the steering wheel caused his knuckles to turn a sickly white.

"First off, the thing ya need to know is that the story I told ya before, about the people coming over in dishes and setting up a city here, was true. That's all thar in the book. What is also in the book is the description of the famine that came over the people and the mangy folks that conjured up the Korrigan in the first place; that's all true too. I do know also that at some point the Korrigan stopped comin'. The book doesn't explain that. Other legends that have been handed down from mouth to mouth, or as they say, in the oral tradition, tell us that there was a lengthy span of time when the beast disappeared altogether; things, ya might say, went back to normal.

"Oh sure, there was the occasional bad seasons where the rain didn't fall like it should, or the fish weren't dragged from the sea as they normally were, but that's normal. It's the circle of life; it's what keeps us on our toes and keeps us thankin' God for the good that we do have. Do ya understand?"

The trio nodded in unison, their features expressing the effort they were using to understand every word delivered from the Captain's mouth.

"The thing ya need to know," he said, turning now to look at Zeke, "is that it came back. It came back because some of *your* relatives," waving his arm around to indicate all three of the children, "went messing around where they shouldn't."

Zeke started to speak, but saw the Captain's warning glare, thought better of it, and closed his mouth, resuming his position next to the window, staring at the now gentle swell that surrounded them.

"I know that this may be hard for ya three to believe, and even harder to accept," he continued. "But as God is my witness, it were those two brothers that got this whole mess started again."

The Captain reached up and pulled back on the throttle, slowing the boat to a stand still. He inched himself off of the helm and squeezed his way past Devon and Taylre. The Captain then climbed down the steps to the deck and began removing fishing supplies from underneath a bench that ran along the inside of the railing. He turned and handed Devon a sturdy fishing pole and began to expertly tie a lure and hook to its thick line while Devon held it steady. When he was done, he took back the pole and cast the line out into the sea. "Fishin' always helps me think," he said as the others looked on. Finally, he turned to the three watchers and motioned with the shrug of his head toward the other poles that were piled on the deck. Each in turn bent and took a fishing rod and tried their best to tie their own lures on the lines.

Taylre, her tongue protruding slightly out of the side of her mouth, expertly spun the stiff line around itself several times while the lure dangled from a small loop she had created. She then used her teeth to secure the knot, tightening the lure down snuggly. Zeke and Devon watched her jealously as they struggled to keep the lure itself from falling off of the line and landing on the deck. As Taylre balanced her fishing pole in a rod holder affixed to the side of the boat, she reached over and began to help Devon and Zeke with their lines, patiently showing them each step of the process. When each line was secure, the boys tossed the lures over the side, letting the lines sink and disappear into the dark murky water. Meanwhile, the heat of the day returned to its former intensity.

After a few moments of watching the lines dip and rise with the waves, the Captain once again resumed his narrative, his pipe continuing to issue forth the sweet scent of tobacco.

"Thar was a time," he began, "many years ago, when your great grandfather was just a little boy, that his family decided it would be best to leave the country of his birth and come to this one. Things there weren't too good. Levi, your great-great grandfather, couldn't find enough work to feed his family. They were livin' in shoddy conditions, in an old shack that leaked whenever it rained, and they barely had enough clothes to cover their backs. Jobs were lackin'. Gathering enough food to feed the family was a struggle, and folks livin' there weren't generally too friendly on account of the bad times. Levi decided he'd had enough and managed to raise a little money to get his family passage on an old, rickety steamboat, where they spent a miserable two weeks crossing the Atlantic ocean.

"When they finally arrived in Halifax, they made their way north to Alder Cove, another arduous journey at the time. Levi went to work on a potato farm helpin out with the chores and bringing in some crops. He was able to scrimp and save some money, and was finally able to buy his own property where he raised his own crops and his family.

"But, as sometimes happens, things don't always work out the way we want them to from year to year. One particular year was very bad. Thar was no rain, the sun beat down like a forger's fire all the time, and what crops there were barely survived. All of the farmers and town's people in Alder Cove struggled to eat that year.

"Well, as the story goes, Levi had himself three strong sons: Leonard, the oldest, Langdon, the next in line, and the youngest of the brood, Nicholas.

"I'm told that Leonard and Langdon, when they grew into their late teens, became a couple of trouble makers. Always in a mess with the law, gettin' drunk in town and findin' themselves in many a fight. They spent quite a few nights in jail, I can tell ya, much to the frustration of the their father, Levi.

"Nicholas, on the other hand, was the apple of his father's eye. He worked hard on the farm, took care of his ailing mother when she contracted the polio and thankfully stayed away from all the drinkin' and fightin' that his brothers seemed to be so fond of; why, he even found himself a beautiful young lass to marry, Evelyn, who eventually gave birth to your grandfather, John Proper."

"The one who died in the ocean," Devon said. "My dad's dad."

"The very same one," the Captain responded, smiling to himself at the distant memory of a dear acquaintance. "He was a damned good man, and a good friend."

"How did it happen?" Zeke asked.

"Well, I'll be gettin to that," he snapped. "I told ya, no questions 'til I'm done with the story."

Zeke cowered slightly at the Captain's sharp response, but tried to ignore it, remembering Taylre's reflection on how the Captain was famous for his short fuse.

Suddenly, Devon unexpectantly dropped his fishing rod and ran to the stern, his complexion turning an intense pale-green, and began to vomit over the back of the boat. With his back turned to the others, Devon's torso could be seen lurching upward in violent pitches. He groaned painfully between each explosion of his breakfast as he clutched tightly onto the railing.

"Shoot for distance, boy," the Captain called, a mischievous grin creeping across his face. "And make sure ya got the wind at your back - ya don't want that comin back at ya." He chuckled to himself and turned back to watching his line rising and falling with the waves, unimpressed and unconcerned.

"Is he okay?" Taylre questioned, a worried expression returning to her face.

"Oh sure," the Captain explained. "He's just got a case of the sea sickness. It'll wear off as soon as we pull in. Anyways, where was I?"

"You were talking about Nicholas and his brothers, how his brothers were dorks but he was a good guy," Zeke answered, still looking over his shoulder at Devon, concerned, but not enough to go over and stand too close to him.

"Dorks," the Captain said thoughtfully. "Well, I suppose that be one way ya could say it, although I'm not sure that'd be the way I'd say it necessarily. Nevertheless, you've got the idea."

From the stern, Devon turned his pathetic, watering eyes toward the group. "Don't go on with the story yet," he moaned, wiping his mouth and nose on a greasy towel he'd found stuck in one of the wooden slats. "I wanna hear what's next."

Devon made his way slowly and painfully back to the others. He sat down heavily on the deck, his back leaning up against the railing. "Okay, go on," he said, waving his hand in a weak gesture toward the Captain.

The Captain smiled feebly and continued. "The two 'dorks', as ya so gently put it," he said, glancing over at Zeke, "were carousing one night with another group of miscreants up along the Stick River."

The Captain stopped his narrative and looked over his shoulder along the shoreline and pointed an accusing finger toward a bridge that lay in the distance, its dark, oily wood contrasting with the dry brown of the landscape surrounding it. "And there it is," he said, almost spitting the words as he uttered them. "The filthy river where the Korrigan slithers up to make her temporary home, waitin to be fed."

All eyes turned to look in the direction of the mouth of the river, a shiver of fear grasping the youths as they stared.

"As the drunkin party made its way along the fields that lined the river, they came across some ancient ruins," the Captain continued. "Apparently, within those ruins they found the book, the original of the copy I now possess. That book contained spells and enchantments. It contained everything they needed to call back the Korrigan - with the promise that if they did, the drought would go away and they would become rich. The land would never be barren, the fish would always be plentiful, and the town would prosper. However, like anything that has to do with the devil and his demons, there's always a price to pay. In this case, the price was a sacrifice."

"A human sacrifice," Taylre said matter-of-factly. "Just like the early Northerners did hundreds of years ago."

"That's right, lass, a human sacrifice. But it had to be the right sacrifice. It couldn't just be anyone, as those lowlifes found out. Why, they went about killing four or five different innocent folks before they decided to read the fine print. That's when they discovered the ritual known as The Selection.

"This ceremony is a sordid affair. It's full of black magic and enough darkness to keep the nightmares comin' for months on end, so I won't go into much detail other than to say it involves circles, smelly burning sticks, little stones with odd writing on them and candles."

Zeke suddenly turned to Taylre. They stared at each other in wonder. The question on their minds was the same: *was the "meeting" that was held in the parlor at Taylre's grandmother's house really The Selection Ceremony? And, were the stones the same ones mentioned in Devon's dream?*

The Captain noticed the curious look that Zeke and Taylre gave one another but pressed on with his story, ignoring the exchange for now. "In this ceremony, the one true sacrifice is revealed. It's then up to the chosen group to find the person, bring him or her to the right location, and give the offerin' to the Korrigan. Once the Korrigan gets the right sacrifice, it leaves and doesn't return for another thirty years."

"Who was it?" Devon asked, his ashen complexion darkening as the pitch and roll of the boat continued. "Who was the eventual sacrifice?"

The Captain turned to look at Devon, somewhat surprised to hear his voice as he had forgotten Devon was even there. "I think you already suspect the answer to that question," the Captain said, reeling in the line and placing the fishing rod back in the storage box. Taylre and Zeke followed suit, reeling in their own lines and gently placing the poles into the stowage.

"The sacrifice was Nicholas," he said solemnly. "They stole him from his small family and sacrificed him for the *good* of the town, at least that's how they would justify it."

"But Captain," Taylre urged, "Wouldn't the police know? Wouldn't somebody've turned them in; let people know that they murdered someone?"

"They made it look like an accident; made up an elaborate story making everyone think he'd been killed at sea. The story was successful, and everybody bought it. They got away with murder. And all of it for power and riches while the innocent suffered.

"That was the first time that the Korrigan returned; thirty years later it came back, just like the book said it would; it came back for its sacrifice, or rather, the cost due for ill begotten riches." The Captain moved toward the helm, climbing the steps carefully and gently, hefting his bulk into the skipper's chair. The trio followed him to the cabin, their anxious minds beginning to piece together some of the lose threads of the sordid tale.

With the Captain comfortably seated, Zeke turned to him. "I really hope that you're not going to say what I think you're going to say," he said.

The Captain turned the key in the ignition and the old diesel that drove the craft roared to life once again. "What is it that ya think I'm going to say, Zeke?" The Captain asked.

"I'm afraid you're going to say that my grandpa was next; that my dad lost his dad to these same kinds of freaks who work in black magic. That's what I'm afraid you're going to say. So please," he begged, "prove me wrong."

The Captain shook his head as he leaned on the throttle and turned the large wheel directing the boat back to the marina. "I wish I could, son, but you're a smart one, all of yas' are," he said, turning to gaze at each of them, "but the truth is, your grandpa died the same way his dad did, through treachery and evil."

"They made it look like an accident too, didn't they?" Devon said. "They told everyone he died at sea, just like they did before."

"Aye, lad, they did."

The old boat sloughed across the water, its engine pushing them sluggishly but consistently toward shore. A deep silence pervaded the cabin where the four sat, each engrossed in their own thoughts. Finally, after a few moments, Taylre spoke up.

"Who is 'they', Captain?" she said, holding firm to a small handle that extended from the sliding door.

"That, I don't know," the Captain said with a sigh. "I have my suspicions, but I can't make any accusations until I know for sure."

"Perhaps it's the sacrifice we should be most worried about right now," Zeke said.

Taylre turned abruptly toward Zeke, a strange look of rage shadowing her face. She began to shake her head violently. "No!" she said, spitting the words forcefully. "No! Don't even say what I think you're going to say."

Zeke stepped back from Taylre, confused, unaware that he'd said anything wrong. He retreated further back, afraid that Taylre may actually strike him. He raised his hands in defense, but the gesture was unnecessary. Instead, Taylre's eyes did the work that any solid punch might do as they seemed to send sharp needles of outrage toward Zeke.

"Here, here now," the Captain said sharply, trying unsuccessfully to step down from the chair and move between Zeke and Taylre. Instead, he used the power of his booming voice to deflect the anger and tension.

Taylre stopped yelling, but her glare told Zeke he was stepping over the line.

"What's this all about?" The Captain asked, shifting his gaze from Taylre to Zeke.
"Zeke, what's going on?"

"Nothing. Actually, I have no idea." Zeke said, looking down, unable to tolerate Taylre's stare any longer.

"There's somethin that's not being said here," the Captain exclaimed, now turning his attention exclusively on Taylre. "Come on young lady, out with it."

Taylre took one more sharp look at Zeke before she turned to the Captain. She sighed in resignation, realizing with reluctance that Zeke was innocent here. Her hasty anger suddenly seemed just as awkward to her as she was sure it did to Zeke. "The ceremony's already been held," she said, now gaining the full attention of the Captain.
"Last night," she said. "Last night there was some sort of secret meeting being held in the parlor. I wasn't allowed access; Mr. Roberts wouldn't let me. He..." she began sobbing. "He said my grandma was busy, and he pushed me to my room. This morning I woke up to find grandma gone. I went over to Zeke and Devon's place and told them what I'd seen."

At this point both Zeke and Devon eagerly piped in and rehashed all that had happened when they went back to Taylre's to investigate. Devon repeated his dream, and Zeke narrated the events that took place in the neighbor's back yard. How Terrance, a frightened teenager, was found mysteriously hunched like a wounded animal in the corner. The Captain listened intently, his mind working vigorously, trying to reconstruct the facts.

"Roberts," he spat. "Roberts was one I didn't suspect, but I should've. Your grandma, I'm sorry to say, I have suspected for some time, both her and the mayor, David Vernon."

"Suspected?" Taylre shouted. "Suspected of what? I was thinking she was the one to be sacrificed!" Zeke looked up in surprise. He suddenly understood Taylre's abrupt display of anger.

The Captain shook his head sadly, "I used to run around with David and Marjorie, your grandma, when I was younger. John, your grandpa," turning to look at Zeke and Devon, "he used to tag along too. However, I always had a suspicion that something sinister was going on; I could never put my finger on it. Now, though, things are becomin very clear. No, Taylre, your grandma isn't the sacrifice she's part of the group of rascals that are tryin' to appease the Korrigan."

Taylre's jaw dropped at the Captain's disclosure. Words could not express her feelings at that moment.

The Captain eased back on the boat's throttle as they drifted into the marina. He expertly guided the craft into its berth, urging each member of the small crew to grab ropes and begin securing the boat to the pier, but only Zeke and Devon helped. Taylre simply stood in shock, trying to wrap her mind around what the Captain had just said.

When the Captain was satisfied that everything was tight and secure aboard the boat, he turned to the kids. "Go home," he ordered. "Go directly to yar house and lock the doors. I've got some business to attend to," he said angrily. Then as an afterthought said, "This Roberts," looking at Taylre, "whar was he standing when ya saw him in your house?"

Taylre thought for just a brief moment, the recollection of the previous night burning painfully in her memory. "Right in front of the parlor door. He was blocking it."

"In front of the door ya say...umm," he said, scratching his whiskers. "My guess is he's the guardian. Well, I'll deal with that when the time comes." He looked sternly at the three. "Get going!"

Zeke, Devon and Taylre jumped at the Captain's thunderous voice and ran. They scrambled along the wooden pier, balancing themselves on the floating docks like tightrope walkers. They continued through the back door of "Typhoon Jacks" and didn't stop until they reached the front door of the Captain's café. Zeke turned the lock and all three exited quickly into the sunshine, shading their eyes against its brightness. As Zeke closed the glass door behind him, he was suddenly jolted by another booming voice.

"Where have you three been!"

Zeke jumped at the bellowing voice and was dismayed to see his father standing next to their car. His father appeared from the shadow of a nearby building, a menacing figure; fury drawn across his face like a black curtain. Zeke then shifted his gaze and noticed the car's windshield was pocked with stars of broken glass and the hood and roof were dented.

"Your mother and I have been worried sick!"

CHAPTER 12

Making Plans

They drove home in tactile silence. Occasionally Mr. Percy Proper's infuriated glare beamed of off the rear-view mirror at the three youths who sat in the backseat, although his anger appeared to be tempered with concern. Zeke, Devon and Taylre sat grimly, wondering what could have possibly made Mr. Proper become so irate, considering he was normally a very quiet, easy-going man, at least until recently.

As they drove through town toward the Proper house, they peered out of the pock-marked windows of the car, their understanding of Mr. Proper's disposition suddenly becoming evident. Driving down Main Street, they could see small businesses, other vehicles, and houses that had their windows and exteriors smashed. People sat on curbs with their heads bound in bandages as ambulance personnel attended to their wounds. Small birds lay dead in the street, as well as some dogs and cats. The destruction of the brief storm was extensive.

When the paneled station wagon pulled up to the Proper house, it stopped abruptly in the driveway. Mr. Proper exited first. The three cousins watched his departure with a kind of relief, as the tension in the vehicle had dissipated too, as if a heavy weight had literally been lifted from the youth's minds, although they knew that it was just a matter of time until they received the full brunt of Mr. Proper's wrath. Finally, the trio exited, but reluctantly. They followed Mr. Proper up the steps and into the house where Mrs. Vivian Proper sat waiting in the kitchen, a cooling cup of coffee sitting in front of her on the table, her eyes streaked with mascara, an obvious sign that she had been crying.

Mrs. Proper rose quickly from her seat and reached for Zeke and Devon first, wrapping them in her arms and hugging them tightly. Then, looking up at Taylre, grabbed her too in a full embrace, the worry on her face beginning to dissolve.

"Have a seat you three," Mr. Proper said, leaning calmly against the kitchen counter. His earlier display of anger softened, but his voice betraying his frustration.

Zeke, Devon and Taylre pulled out chairs from the kitchen table and sat, but within each of them, a tight ball of worried anticipation was tightening.

"We've tried to give you as much freedom as possible," Mr. Proper began with a sigh, "but perhaps we've given too much. Your mom and I have been huddled inside the house terrified of the horrible weather we've just experienced; terrified because it was hailing large chunks of ice everywhere, but also because we didn't know where you three were. You must have seen all of the destruction that it caused in the town. Didn't you see the broken glass, the dented cars and the dead animals?" Then added, "And now there's talk of a boy missing. Who knows, he may have been hit by one of those chunks of falling ice and is now lying dead somewhere."

Vivian Proper, who was silent up until now, spoke up. "Where were you? What were you doing?"

Zeke looked about him, seeing that his companions were remaining mute. He looked up at his mom and dad, realizing that he would have to be the spokesman. "We were with the Captain," Zeke said. "We were on his boat in the marina when the storm came, but we were safe inside, nobody got hurt."

"The Captain?" Percy Proper said incredulously, pushing himself away from the counter. "You mean you were with Bartholomew Gunner?"

The three looked at each other and shrugged, they had never heard of Bartholomew Gunner before. "I guess so," Zeke said. "We just know him as the Captain."

Percy Proper inhaled deeply and breathed out a sharp sigh. "If I'd known you were with Bartholomew Gunner all this time, I would have never let you out," he said harshly. "That old goat is the biggest bag of hot air this town has ever had. I suppose he's been filling your heads with all sorts of stories and rumors. Let me guess," Percy continued, his anger once again mounting. "He probably told you there's a monster that roams around here eating people."

The children sat staring at Mr. Proper, their mouths hanging open in shock.

Percy shook his head in dismay, seeing the dumbfounded look on the three faces gaping up at him. "He did, didn't he? What else did he tell you? That the town's cursed, that there's a secret group of devil worshippers that meet to plot the destruction of the town? Well, if he did, and I'm sure he did, I don't want you believing any of it. He's been telling those stories for years. He was telling them even when I was a kid living here."

"But," Taylre interjected, "he said that your dad..."

"My dad," Percy Proper interrupted, a piercing look in his eyes, "died in a storm while he was out fishing. There is no monster, there is no secret society, and there is no secret book. Anything that the *Captain* said about any of those things is simply not true and I forbid you to see or talk to that man anymore. Do you understand?"

Percy Proper glared at the three as they bowed their heads, Devon fidgeted with a fold of his shirt, Taylre sat seemingly engrossed in a split end that she found in her hair, and Zeke twiddled his thumbs. "Yes, Sir," Zeke finally said, the other two nodding awkwardly.

"Good," Percy said, leaning back on the kitchen counter. "Now, we have a lot of clean up to do around here. The storm has broken a lot of windows, especially the two along the east side of the garage. I have some gloves in the garage in a box marked 'garden supplies', go find them and start cleaning up the glass and whatever small branches may have been knocked loose around the outside of the house. Be careful though; I don't want you getting cut."

Vivian Proper then leaned in hesitantly, her voice an odd mixture of exasperation and calm. "Taylre, we've been trying to get a hold of your grandma but we can't seem to. Do you know where she might be? I'm sure she's quite worried about you, too."

"I'm...I'm not sure," she stuttered, looking first at Zeke then back at Mrs. Proper. "Maybe she's at work. I haven't seen her all day."

"I tried calling her there, just so she would know that we were looking for you," Vivian Proper added, "But I couldn't reach her there either. In fact, I couldn't reach anyone at the town's offices, which seemed a bit odd. But maybe they're all helping with the cleanup of the town. We'll try to reach her later. The important thing is that you're safe now."

Percy Proper moved inconspicuously to the far end of the kitchen and poured himself a fresh cup of coffee, his eyes shifting nervously at the mention of Taylre's grandmother and the mention of the unusual vacancy of the town offices.

When the tension in the room calmed to a sustainable level, the trio left Percy and Vivian Proper standing in the kitchen. They gathered in the garage to begin their assigned jobs, their heads swimming with conflicting thoughts. Devon separated himself immediately and rummaged through boxes while Taylre sifted among the littered remains of old discarded newspapers used to wrap delicate items. Zeke stood defiantly near the door to the garage, his arms crossed, a scowl drawn over his face.

"What in the name of all that's holy are you two doing?" Zeke said, glaring at his companions.

Devon and Taylre looked up innocently from their distractions and stared at Zeke. "What do you mean?" Devon answered. "We're looking for gloves, just like dad told us to do. What are you doing?"

"I, my goofy looking little brother, am trying to solve a mystery. Or, have you forgotten what we started to get accomplished today?" Zeke said shrewdly.

"I," Devon said, mimicking Zeke, "am doing what I was told to do. Not standing around with my finger up my nose, ignoring my dad's demand like you are."

Zeke pulled out a folded piece of paper from his pocket, smoothed it open on the edge of a nearby table and held it out for Devon and Taylre to see. "Do you recall the list?" he questioned emphatically, thrusting the page toward the faces of Taylre and Devon. "Everything written here so far shows that there *is* something going on around here - the dreams, the pictures, Terrance, the meeting - all of it."

"But dad told us..." Devon began.

"Forget about dad!" Zeke roared, and then quickly brought his hand up to his mouth to shush himself, at the same time peering over his shoulder, hoping that neither Percy nor Vivian Proper had heard his shout. Then in a softer, more subdued voice added, "it's all here in black and white. There's something up. We can't ignore the facts. And let's not forget what happened in your house today, Taylre. You can't tell me you've already forgotten *that* little incident?"

Taylre nodded her head slowly as the vivid memory of a black apparition descending from the ceiling filled her thoughts once more. "No," she whispered. "I haven't forgotten."

"And you, Devon. You couldn't even stay in the house because of the way you felt. Do you remember that?" Zeke inquired, directing a dagger-like stare at his little brother.

Devon paused for a moment, considering the implications of Zeke's words, and then he too nodded his head, but added, "What about dad? He seemed convinced that the Captain had no idea what he was talking about. Maybe there is nothing to his stories. Maybe dad's right and we should just let the whole thing go."

"Let it go! Let it go? No, we've got to see this thing through. We've got to get to the bottom of what's really happening," Zeke proclaimed.

"If we proceed," Taylre said, a lone figure standing among a pile of discarded papers, "then how do we go about it? You heard your dad, he doesn't want us to have anything to do with the Captain. Are you willing to just disobey him and follow the Captain around anyway?"

"No," Zeke answered confidently. "That ship has sailed. I think that we have gotten all of the information that we can get from the Captain. It's up to us now to put it all together. Once we've done that, then we can move on."

Zeke looked over the paper again, his gaze searching the list, and laid it out on a tool bench. He searched among his father's scattered tools and found a carpenter's pencil. The tip was dull, so, rummaging some more, Zeke found one of his father's old pocket knives and began sharpening the end of the pencil to a fine point. With the writing utensil in hand he began to add, in his skilled handwriting, more entries to the group's record.

His last entry was number four:
4.   Strange meeting - grandma gone all night.

Zeke read it out loud and looked up for confirmation from the others. They nodded briefly, and then he added number five:
5.   **Evil presence in Taylre's house - may be The Selection Ceremony.**

Again, he read the entry and looked up. This time Taylre spoke up. "Don't forget to put down that grandma is still missing." Then she added, "and just for the record, I'm not convinced about what the Captain said about grandma, I can't believe she'd be mixed up in something like this. And you wouldn't either if you knew her."

Zeke added some notes beside the number five and then penciled in number six:
6. **Stones mentioned in Devon's dream and also mentioned as part**
    of ceremony - nothing about stones in Captain's book.

"This is where we get stuck," Zeke said. "I think before we go any further, we've got to locate this other book, if, in fact, there is one."

"Finding the other book, or anything about the stones, will be hard, especially since we haven't got a clue where to start," Devon added.

"Perhaps there's something else to consider first," Taylre said, tapping the side of her chin with her forefinger in a thoughtful pose. "Think about the last words the Captain said. Remember he told us that he had some business to take care of? Then he asked me about Mr. Roberts? He asked me where he was standing; when I told him, he said something about Roberts being a guardian, whatever that is. Do you remember?"

Zeke nodded enthusiastically. "And, he showed us the river; the one that he claimed the Korrigan swam up when ever it came to Alder Cove. There had to be some significance there."

"Wait a minute. Just wait a minute," Devon piped in. "Think about what you're saying and then think about what dad said: there is no monster, there is no secret anything - he said so. And he said that the Captain was a storyteller. What if he's right and the Captain is just pulling our leg."

"Do we have to remind you again of what you've seen and felt, Devon? Keep in mind, you are the one that had the dreams, not us. It would seem to me that you, little brother, are scared, but we all are. However, that doesn't change the fact that the things on this list are reality. We've got to pursue them, because if we don't, nobody else will." Zeke slammed the pencil on the table with finality, looking at Devon with a don't-you-dare-contradict-me stare.

"I agree," Taylre said. This time Devon looked up in surprise. It wasn't so long ago that Taylre was begging them not to continue this particular adventure, now, incredibly, she was agreeing with Zeke. "I also think I might know where the Captain is going to take care of this so-called business," Taylre exclaimed, her confidence making her stand a little straighter. "I think he's heading to the river. I think," she paused, looking from Zeke to Devon, "he's heading to where he *thinks* the Korrigan might be so that *he* can stop it."

As Taylre's words struck Devon, he turned, frantically looking about the messy garage for a chair to sit on. He found an old, weathered and torn patio chair that his mom had set out to be thrown into the garbage, and he sat down heavily, his bottom pushing through the worn fabric almost causing him to end up on the floor, but the material held. As he sat glumly, he looked up at the two enthusiastic faces staring down at him. "I'm not going with you," he said, his head cradled in his hands.

"Going?" Zeke asked. "Are we going somewhere?"

"You're going to the river to help the Captain. Don't deny it. That's what you were both thinking. You're both planning on sneaking out and heading to the river, and I'm telling you, I'm not going. Don't ask me why; just know that I'm not going." Devon said with finality.

Taylre and Zeke both turned and looked at each other at the same time. Their expressions were ones of mild surprise. They knew that Devon had recently displayed an eerie way of sensing things, but this time Devon had perceived their thoughts before they even thought them; that left them both a little shaken.

"Okay," Zeke whispered. "You stay here. You can make sure neither mom nor dad gets suspicious about where we've gone. Make sure that you keep your window open so we can climb back in. Does that sound alright?"

"That sounds fine," Devon responded in a hushed voice. "Just be careful. I have a really bad feeling about this."

"We will," Taylre assured him.

Zeke glanced about the garage and noted that the late afternoon light piercing through the one broken window was fading. He walked over to the small window that was framed by the aging garage door and looked out into the street. Evening would be falling shortly; he sensed that both he and Taylre should get a move on before it got too dark. He, too, had a feeling that they did not want to be caught out near the river past nightfall.

The three made a quick turn around the house and the garage, giving the impression that they were cleaning up broken glass and fallen branches as they had been told to do. Occasionally, one of them picked up a broken limb or two and tossed it into the wood pile, making it look like they were working hard, but in fact their minds were focused on the adventure at hand and the possible dangers that it held.

When they were sure that they had made a good enough impression of cleaning up the glass, the trio noisily entered through the back door and clomped their way up the stairs into Devon's room. As an added assurance, Zeke slammed the bedroom door making sure that his mom and dad heard them enter the room. Then, in a loud conspicuous voice Zeke said, "Why sure, Taylre, we'd love to play a long game of monopoly," drawing out each syllable, making sure that his parents could hear every word.

When Zeke was sure all was secure, he turned and locked the door. He started to move toward the window when he heard a gentle scratching from the other side of the door. He returned, unlocked it, and found Rufus standing in the hallway, his tail wagging eagerly. With barely a thought, Rufus slipped quickly through the small opening Zeke had provided, trod lightly across the bare wooden floor, and climbed up on Devon's bed where he circled three times, sniffed once around the edges of the pillow, then curled himself up into a tight ball, immediately falling asleep.

Zeke ignored the intrusion and continued his way toward the window, peering out and down into the backyard. Feeling his way around the edges of the wooden framed window pane, Zeke began to pick away at the crusted paint that held the window fast. After clearing the frame of debris, Zeke pushed upward releasing a slight grunt with the effort. Reluctantly, the window slid up, making a sharp squeal that made Taylre cringe as the noise seemed to pierce into her mouth and vibrate off of her braces. Its protests being ineffectual, the window opened, but only barely. Zeke was just able to put his head through the opening, but it was enough for him to see the entire backyard as well as a perfect view of the side of the house. Looking down, he saw that the earlier occupants had built a latticework frame in order to support some now withered vines, but this, Zeke could see, was a perfect spot to climb down safely from the window. He waved Taylre over and showed her the frame. She confidently nodded her approval and a strategy was quickly formulated.

Devon, watching the two make their plans, sat at his small desk in the corner of the room. He pulled out the tightly folded piece of paper that he stowed in one of the drawers and stared once again at the evil drawing he had completed earlier, the memory of the dream and its frightful reality brushing his nerves like nails on a chalkboard. He looked up again and saw Zeke and Taylre preparing to descend the makeshift ladder. As Taylre disappeared through the window into the fading light of evening, Zeke lifted his body through the window opening and began his descent. As he shifted out of the window, Rufus, stirred from his nap, lifted his head, watching intently as Zeke disappeared into the fading light. As Zeke was about to drop out of sight he stopped and stuck his head back in through the window, looking directly and intently at Devon, his expression filled with rare concern. "We'll be alright," he said, a note of tenderness in his voice. "Just make sure you keep the window open. We'll try to be back before it gets too dark. And don't forget, you've got to keep mom and dad distracted. If we get caught, we'll all be in for it." Then he smiled gently and vanished into the late afternoon just like the light that filled Devon's room and his disturbed thoughts.

CHAPTER 13

John Proper

Each time he pulled on the rope, the small engine that sat perched on the back of the tiny fishing boat grumbled, sputtered, and then died. Beads of sweat dribbled down the back of the Captain's neck, over his bushy eyebrows, into his eyes, and down the middle of his back. His breathing came in heavy bursts as he tried frantically to make the ancient motor start. He checked the gas again, fiddled with the sparkplug and continually adjusted the choke back and forth, but still the stubborn Evinrude outboard motor refused to fire up. He sat down heavily on the wooden bench seat and toweled himself dry, gulping down water from a camp canteen. He cursed quietly under his breath and reconsidered the hunt he was about to embark upon.

He scanned the floor of the old 12 ft. fishing boat, noting the coiled length of rope, a large sheathed hunting knife, a box of twelve gauge shot gun shells and an outdated double barrel shot gun - a weapon that he'd received as a birthday present when he was fifteen years old from his father. He picked it up tenderly, caressing the smooth, black metal barrel and examined the polished surface of the wooden stock. He hefted its weight, feeling the precision balance of the gun and considered the use he would soon put it to, assuming, of course, he could get the small engine started and begin making his way southward toward the mouth of the river. He gently placed the firearm back down on the floor of the boat and once again began pulling at the rope.

The engine, though reluctant to start, stuttered, choked, almost died, but then sputtered again, built up momentum, puffed out a torrent of black smoke, and roared into life. The Captain reached down quickly and adjusted the choke, which caused the racing engine to slow its idle and calm to a pleasant rumble. The Captain smiled to himself.

"I knew she'd go eventually," he said, turning toward the front of the craft while his right hand guided the swivel of the outboard. The Captain steered the boat out into the marina, aiming it past the larger fishing vessels and sailboats that sat idle in their berths and directed it toward open water. He followed the coastline in a southerly direction riding the gentle swells as the small motor puttered along easily.

The open sea was calm which made the trip toward the river's mouth smooth going. Captain Bartholomew Gunner sat upright, the glare of the sun reflecting off the water shining brilliantly onto his face and baldhead. He closed his eyes and felt the warm breeze touch his face like a lover's caress. The ocean was his home, and it was here, on the waves, where the salt wind tickled his senses that he felt almost comfortable. Yet it was also on this same sea that the Captain felt a contradiction of emotions: respect for its vastness, and fear for the harbingers of evil that used its resources for their own corrupt pleasures.

As he allowed the fresh breeze to brush his face, a sense of reverie enveloped him, sending his thoughts back thirty years to a cool, moonless night. The memory brought back the utter exhaustion that both he and John Proper had felt from the long day's work hauling in net after net that held their hopes and dreams, but no fish. That day had been filled with disappointment. It seemed as if the fish had dried up, simply vanished just like the land and the tourists around Alder Cove. They felt that their labors were in vain as they tried to make a meager living from the sea.

Bartholomew remembered John as a calloused, determined worker. He also recalled that John could be moody and prone to outbursts of sudden anger, his bright green eyes reflecting displeasure in simple mistakes made by himself and those around him. However, he was quick to forgive others their mistakes, but struggled to forgive himself for his wrongdoings. Nevertheless, there were times when he could be so cheerful that his laugh and smile were infectious. On this particular day, however, John's mood was as dark as the water they drifted on and Bartholomew knew from experience that it was best to keep his distance; he just let John deal with his bleak disposition and hope it ended quickly.

Fatigued from the day's work, the two men readied themselves for a short rest. The first light of morning would see the men up again pursuing the elusive catch, but sleep was first needed to renew their strength.

John, frustrated from the lack of fish and worried for his small family who remained at home in Alder Cove, settled into a restless slumber on a rickety chair above deck while Bartholomew snuggled into a weary unconsciousness in a bunk below.

While the two men napped, another boat, its lights off and its motor rumbling at a low idle, sidled up, bumping them gently on the starboard side. Bartholomew stirred uneasily in his sleep, but paid no attention to the noise, passing it off as a simple movement of the boat.

In the moonless dark, a small assembly of cloaked and hooded figures exited their vessel and stepped over the railings onto the deck of John and Bartholomew's boat. Their stealth movements were as smooth as oozing sludge. The sinister group surrounded John Proper's sleeping figure and in one motion lifted him from the chair that he dozed in, causing him to awaken with a start. An unknown mysterious figure placed a hand roughly across John's mouth as he tried to call out, but all that escaped was a muffled cry. Then, John Proper was violently thrown onto the deck of the other waiting boat while another group of hooded figures encircled him. They applied tape over his mouth, ropes around his hands and feet, and carried him below deck as the dark craft gently pulled away, leaving Bartholomew Gunner fast asleep in his bunk far below deck.

In the early morning light, a slight breeze began to agitate the sea. The waves started to rise and the boat jostled with the moving water. Bartholomew tossed uncomfortably in his cot, licking his dry lips and tasting the salt that clung to his skin. He rose sleepily from his slumber and swung his tired legs to the floor. As his feet touched the smooth surface, he immediately had an odd sensation. The air seemed to close in about him and his stomach lurched with nausea. He shook his head trying to eliminate the feeling that began to overwhelm him while rubbing his unshaven face vigorously. He was not prone to seasickness, yet the feeling he was experiencing seemed to fit the symptoms. He stood unsteadily, bracing himself momentarily on a nearby table when suddenly he knew why he was feeling ill. He didn't understand, but he just knew something very wrong had happened, as if he were unexpectedly the recipient of extra sensory perception.

He climbed the steep stairs leading to the deck and the open air, throwing open the door like a frenzied man, his eyes searching wildly for something, anything that might be amiss. Immediately, his eyes rested on the toppled chair where John had slumbered the night before. It lay on its side, one of the wooden arms splintered. A blanket, its tasseled ends flapping with the slight gusts of wind, sat disheveled next to the upended chair, but John was nowhere to be seen.

At first, Bartholomew assumed the worst: John, his depression getting the best of him, had reduced himself to suicide and tossed himself overboard. But Bartholomew knew better. He knew that John was not capable of such an action. Instead, he searched his thoughts and realized that his suspicions of David Vernon, Marjorie Proper, and the others was probably correct, and that something foul and evil had happened here last night while he slept. He fell to his knees as hot tears flowed freely, feeling pain and anguish course through his body. His fear of what may have happened to his friend caused him to let out a howl of grief and helplessness.

As these distant memories faded from the Captain's mind, the hand that guided the old outboard motor reached up to wipe away fresh tears. Tears that reminded the Captain of the loss of a friend, of an evil that need not be, but mostly of his own cowardice for not doing something, *anything* to avenge his friend's death and to put an end to the hold that these wicked people had on the town and its occupants.

Gently plodding through the waves in the old fishing boat, the Captain realized that now was the time to put away his fear and face the evil. In the back of his mind, he worried that he had no idea how to rid the town of the blackness, but he knew that he could wait no longer; if *he* didn't do it, who else would?

Eventually, after an hour of sailing the length of the coast, the Captain came in sight of the mouth of the Stick River, its brown silt dissipating into the dark blue of the sea. He turned the bow toward the river, its opening gaping open like the jaws of a hungry monster waiting to be fed. Upon seeing the river, its narrow banks meandering toward the hills in the distance, a shiver of fear ran up and down his spine causing him to rethink his decision to begin this battle, but his determination overran his dread and he pushed forward.

The small outboard engine continued to cough and sputter as the Captain guided the boat underneath the wooden bridge. As he passed into the momentary shade of the overpass and then once again into the sunshine, the Captain felt as if he had just crossed over a threshold into the realm of no return.

The late afternoon was receding and the bright light of day was fading; nevertheless, the heat continued to bear down. Bartholomew wiped beads of sweat from his brow with a ragged towel then drained the last of his water in one final gulp. He turned his attention to the narrow path of water and the distant thicket of trees that lay in the distance, knowing that the tiny forest that banked the river would be his final destination. However, what waited for him there left him uncertain and nervous.

Dragging his hand in the coolness of the river, the Captain noted how the light that should have reflected off its surface seemed to be sucked down into its depths like a vacuum. He brought his hand out of the water, splashing cool droplets onto his neck and arms, a momentary relief from the heat. Looking up from his wooden bench the Captain discovered he was making good progress toward his goal. Then, rounding a turn in the river he saw a sign perched on the end of a rusted metal stake sticking out of the dry bank, its ominous message almost shouting its threat: **Danger Ahead - Do Not Enter - Private Property.** The Captain ignored the sign's admonition and charged on, setting his jaw into a stiff, determined pose. He sailed around another turn in the river and suddenly saw, standing on a bit of rock that jutted out over the water, Mr. Roberts, clothed in a black suit, his arms crossed over his chest, his black hair stirring in the warm breeze. Roberts stared menacingly at the Captain, yet his mouth was turned up faintly in an evil grin, his lips slightly parted, revealing gleaming white teeth.

He raised his hands into the air as if he were summoning the wind to blow and the sky to fall. His head lifted too and he began to shout as if the river and the fields were his congregation of devoted listeners. "'For ye were as sheep going astray; but are now returned unto the shepherd and bishop of your soul!'"

He lowered his hands and arms, then he smiled, his pale, chapped lips outlining an evil grin; his eyes revealing nothing but scorn. "We've been waiting for you, Bartholomew," Roberts said calmly, his pasty skin outlining the black depthless eyes that mirrored a kind of pleasure in his taunt.

"Yes, Bartholomew, we've been waiting a long time, almost thirty-years now. It's good of you to finally show up."

CHAPTER 14

Vantage Point

Devon woke suddenly from a restless, dreamless sleep. His right arm, which had been propped behind his head, ached and tingled after having been placed in its awkward position for so long. A small pool of drool had accumulated on his pillow. He quickly wiped away the remainder of his spit from the side of his face as he slowly sat up. The comic book he had been reading fluttered to the floor beside his bed.

He turned to look at the clock radio that rested on his night stand, its numbers glowing an eerie red in the darkness of the room. Noting the time, Devon realized that Zeke and Taylre had been gone for just over an hour. He stood up on the cool hardwood floor and made his way over to the lightswitch when he heard a noise coming from outside his window. Rufus, who was resting on the bed beside Devon, lifted his head at the sound and began to whine.

"It's okay, boy," Devon said, reassuring the dog with a gentle pat on the head. "It's probably just Zeke coming home."

He turned without switching on the light and moved toward the open window, just as Zeke had requested. When he reached the window, he again heard a sound, the banging of the trellis against the side of the house, as someone began to climb its wooden slats to the opening above. Devon leaned out and looked down expecting to see either Zeke or Taylre making their way up the makeshift ladder. Instead, Devon was surprised to see three dark, hooded figures climbing toward him, their features covered entirely by their hoods and the dark of the evening.

As the first of the shaded figures approached the opening, Devon reared back in fright, his eyes wide and his breathing coming in rapid, halting exhalations. Devon fell back against the bed and Rufus began to bark, his normally calm temperament changing to a protective, defensive animal. A black-cloaked figure entered the room through the window; another quickly followed him. They moved menacingly toward Devon, their arms outstretched in an attempt to encircle their intended victim. Rufus jumped down from the bed, his teeth bared and the hair on his back, near the base of his shoulders, standing on end. He crouched in front of Devon protectively as a low growl murmured from deep within his throat. Suddenly, Rufus let out a yelp of pain and fell to the floor, struggling to rise, but unable to gain his balance as his legs wobbled uncontrollably and his eyes fought the urge to close.

Devon let out a sharp cry as he witnessed his dog's unusual behavior. He turned to look toward the window where another cloaked figure stood with a small weapon pointed at the fallen animal. "If you come peacefully," the shadowed man at the window said, his voice rough and raspy, "then we won't have to use the same kind of force on you. However, if you resist, make no mistake, I won't hesitate to put a tranquilizer in your neck as well."

* * * * *

Small pieces of dirt flew up from the over-sized back tires on Taylre's bike as she peddled frantically on the back roads that edged the southern part of the town. Zeke struggled to keep up discovering that Taylre rode her bike as quickly and efficiently as she ran. Occasionally, a rock would fly up from her back tire and whiz past his face, but quick reflexes always saved him from a stone to the head.

The two had been traveling the smooth dirt and gravel paths for nearly an hour, making their way through the darkening neighborhoods; finally passing into the farmlands and tree lined foothills. Zeke was thankful to have Taylre as his guide, realizing that he would have been completely lost without her direction.

They rode swiftly and easily over the dirt road, gently rising over an incline and coming to a skidding halt in front of a metal gate. A faded yellow sign pocked with small caliber bullet holes was bolted to a metal gate. Its message seemed to shout a warning that could hardly be ignored: **DO NOT ENTER-PRIVATE PROPERTY.** Zeke read the sign and was dismayed by its implications. "Now what do we do?" he asked Taylre, struggling to catch his breath as he wiped away the sweat that trickled down the sides of his face in small rivulets.

Taylre jumped off her bike and pushed it over to the chain-link fence that connected to the gate. She leaned her bike against it and stepped confidently toward the gate's opening. "We go through," she responded. Then, handing Zeke her glasses said, "Here, hold these. I'll never get my head through with them on."

She grasped a small metal handle and tugged at the gate. It swung out a few inches, but was then stopped by a thick chain and an enormous padlock. Zeke watched as Taylre expertly knelt down just under the chain and the lock and then managed to squeeze herself between the narrow opening, passing through to the other side. Zeke's mouth dropped open a few inches as he realized what an amazing feat she had just accomplished. "There is no way that I will be able to do that," he exclaimed.

"Not if you don't try," she said. "Now, get down and push yourself through. The hardest part is the head. Once that passes through, it's a piece of cake. The rest will just follow."

"What if I just climbed the fence? Wouldn't that be easier?"

Taylre looked upward and Zeke's eyes followed her gaze noting the razor wire and barbed wire that was connected to the top of the fence line. "Looks like somebody really wants to keep people out. Are you sure we should be going this way?"

"This is the quickest way to the river, unless we go out to the highway and walk in from the bridge, but that's a long way. We'd be walking until midnight."

Zeke shrugged his shoulders, leaned his own bike against the fence, took in a deep breath and crouched down under the chain. Taylre leaned in to the gate, pushing with all of her strength in an attempt to make the opening as large as possible for Zeke to squeeze through. Zeke began by shoving his forehead into the notch, feeling the metal bite into his flesh. He grimaced at the pain but continued to push as Taylre spoke encouraging words while still straining against the gate. Finally, with a shot of pain and one last effort, Zeke managed to poke his head through, a trickle of blood sliding down the side of his face. He then turned his body to the left, allowing his shoulder to slip through which was followed by his upper torso. With that portion of his body through, it was easy for Zeke to pull his legs and feet the rest of the way. When he was finally on the other side, Taylre relaxed as well, her muscles spent from the exertion.

"See," she said gleefully. "That wasn't so bad, was it?"

Zeke dabbed the spot of blood that stained his left temple and started to apply pressure to the minor wound with the heel of his hand. Taylre stepped forward with a sweaty handkerchief that she pulled from her back pocket and began to wipe away the blood, its flow already beginning to coagulate. Zeke gratefully accepted the first aid, taking the handkerchief from Taylre and finishing the clean up.

Zeke turned back to the small opening he had just squeezed through, marveling that he was able to pass. He took a quick sideways glance at Taylre and wondered if his head was really that much bigger. He imagined that someday he might have a head the same size as the Captain's.

"What do we do with those?" he asked, coming back to the present and noticing the two bikes leaning up against the fence on the other side, unlocked and unprotected.

"We leave them. There's no way they'll fit through. From here on out it's all on foot."

"But, won't somebody steal them?" Zeke inquired worriedly.

"Nobody comes out here. Trust me. Those bikes will be safe," Taylre assured.

Zeke looked up at the small bullet holes that marred the yellow sign and questioned Taylre's confidence. Then he tried to hand the bloodied handkerchief back to her, but Taylre just shook her head. "You keep it. Just in case it starts to bleed again."

Zeke stuck the stained cloth in his back pocket and began to follow Taylre across an overgrown field of dried, prickly weeds, a faded path barely visible in the dimming light.

The two cousins followed the path in a straight line, continuing a gentle rise to the top of a small hill. When they reached the top, Taylre, who was in the lead, suddenly stopped, bent down low to the ground and pulled at Zeke's shirtfront, bidding him too to stoop next to her. Zeke, propping himself up slightly on his elbows, crept up closely beside Taylre like a soldier crawling under barbed wire fortifications, and noted the look of fear in her expression, her face turning paler than usual.

"What is it?" he said, peering down the slope on the opposite side of the hill.

"There," she whispered sharply, pointing with her index finger toward a small but dense stand of trees near the river.

Zeke's eyes followed her finger noticing the brown dry grass that mottled the slope of the hill leading down to the river's bank, and the amber light that the fading sun left. He also noted the thickness of the small clump of trees next to the river and how odd it was that the leaves which filled the branches were thick and green, so unlike the surrounding area. Their deep shadows seemed to pervade the area with an ominous foreboding. His eyes then found a small camp fire that burned brightly near the bank of the river next to a rectangular mound of rocks. As his eyes adjusted to the dark, he made out shapes moving amongst the blackness, casting their own shadows as they wandered near the flickering fire light. Suddenly, he saw the thing that made Taylre's face turn so pale. The thing that caused Zeke too, to tremble inside and make the hair on the back of his neck stand on end. Near the river's edge and just out of the camp fire's light sat a lone figure, his back facing Zeke and Taylre. However, the curve of his thick neck, his bald, gleaming head in the flickering firelight, his thick arms that were tied tightly behind his back with the same rope that he'd thrown in the bottom of his boat that very afternoon, and the tattoo of an anchor and eel that seemed to weep with a river of sweat that oozed down his arms, identified the captive as none other than the Captain.

Zeke's neck muscles began to tighten. His hands curved into raging fists; the sight of the Captain, his helpless, beaten down form was too much for Zeke to take. He began to rise from his position in the dried grass, slowly bringing himself into a kneeling position. His muscles tensed and flexed, ready to run.

"*What are you doing*? Taylre said, grabbing hold of Zeke's shirt front and once again forcefully pulling him down to the hardened, dusty ground.

"I'm going down to get the Captain," he spat, eyeing her angrily, although his fury was directed elsewhere.

"You'll get yourself killed, or worse, you'll get yourself, me, *and* the Captain killed. This is no time to be a hero."

"But look at him," Zeke stammered. "He's...he's.."

"A captive. I know. But our best bet right now is to take a close look at the situation. We've got to consider the options before we rush down there and get ourselves involved in something that is way over our heads."

Taylre's calming words began to reassure Zeke and he slowly relaxed, though he remained alert and guarded. He eased himself back down to a lying posture on the crest of the hill, his elbows tucked under his chest allowing his head to be slightly elevated.

"Take a look down there," Taylre said, using her chin as a pointer. "There are several hooded people walking around while others are sitting or standing close to the fire. There's one person over by that stone table, and another one just beyond the stand of trees looking out over the river. The problem is, we can't determine who they are; it's just too dark."

"So what do we do?" Zeke said. "We can't wait here all night hoping they'll come up here and introduce themselves."

"There's no need to get sarcastic, monkey boy," Taylre said, looking guiltily at Zeke from the corner of her eye. "Sorry. I guess Devon's starting to rub off on me a little."

"Not a good thing, trust me. You do not want to be in league with that guy," he said, leaning in to her slightly, recognizing her attempt at a joke.

"But you're right," she continued. "We can't wait here all night. Maybe our best bet is to head back and tell the police what's going on. This is definitely a case of kidnapping."

As she spoke, Zeke's attention was only partially on her voice, the other half was on watching the moving shapes below as they appeared to be waiting for something. Suddenly, Zeke gasped and gripped hard onto Taylre's arm. Now it was his turn to point. As he did, Taylre followed the direction of his anxious gaze and saw a man approach the Captain and force him to his knees. The Captain turned, facing in the direction of the children, his face bruised and bloodied, but his expression resolute. The man who forced the Captain to his knees had his back toward Zeke and Taylre and oddly enough, as the two cousins noted, the man did not wear a hooded robe, but rather a black suit, his head bare, his black slicked hair gleaming in the flicker of firelight.

It was Taylre's turn to gasp as she suddenly recognized the figure. She found herself involuntarily scuttling herself backward in the dirt and grass, as if she were being attacked by a slithering snake.

"What is it!" Zeke whispered sharply.

"Ro...Roberts..." She stammered. "That's Mr. Roberts sta..standing over the...the Captain!"

"Roberts?" Zeke exclaimed. "But I thought you said -"

"Never mind what I said!" Taylre said harshly. "That's Roberts, there's no question about it." Taylre breathed deeply, panting slightly as she tried to regain her composure. After a few moments, she inched herself forward, peering down again at Mr. Roberts who stood over the Captain waving his arms and expostulating some well rehearsed sermon.

"But if that's Roberts," Zeke said questionably, "Then who are those other people standing around?"

Now, both Zeke and Taylre found themselves inching their way even further along the rough ground hoping to catch a better glimpse of the hooded figures who waited by the fire. As they approached, Taylre stopped abruptly, gripping the ground firmly in her hands, anger replacing any sense of fear she may have harbored.

"It's her," she said, her voice taking on an eerie quality.

"Who?" whispered Zeke.

"My grandmother. And, over there, standing next to her, the Mayor, David Vernon. They're all in on it. Every one of them...in on it."

"In on what?" Zeke questioned.

"Whatever it is that's going on here," Taylre responded, her voice cracking a little with the pain of her discovery. "I can't believe she would do this...my own grandmother. The Captain was right."

Zeke stared at Taylre in disbelief as the gravity of the situation began to show itself to him. He slowly brought himself up to his knees and tugged at the back of Taylre's shirt, urging her to follow him back to the crest of the hill. When they arrived and situated themselves in a secure position, Zeke placed his arm around Taylre's shoulders trying his best to comfort her.

The light of day had almost completely faded now and the illumination from the small fire seemed to brighten the faces of those who stood near it. "That's Chief Walford," Taylre noted, using her chin again as a pointer. "The policeman we saw in the backyard when Terrance was hurt. They're all here, all of the people who run this town...they're all here...all in on it."

"In on what, though?" Zeke said. "That's the mystery we've got to figure out. Does it all have to do with the book in the Captain's locker? Do these people really think there's some truth to this monster thing?"

Just as Zeke and Taylre began to process the meaning of the strange evening, a sudden flash from a spotlight mounted atop a small fishing boat could be seen on the river making its way toward the stand of trees. The two cousins crouched further back as if the searching lights might locate them and expose their hiding place. The boat moved slowly and stealthily along the narrow inlet, its skipper keeping it in the center of the river until it reached a place close to where Mr. Roberts stood. But before Roberts moved to catch the toss of the rope offered by one of the sailors, he lifted his foot and shoved the Captain roughly, back to a semi-seated position, causing the Captain to round his back and jut his feet out in an effort to maintain his balance.

The occupants of the small craft threw the length of rope to Roberts which he easily caught and then tied deftly to a mangled trunk of a dead, ancient tree. Two hooded figures lifted a bound object over the side of the boat and placed it in the outstretched arms of Mr. Roberts.

The small group standing around the fire, including Marjorie Anders and the Mayor, set out en masse toward the makeshift landing where the motley group of dark figures exited the boat. They proceeded to congregate around the package that Roberts held when it suddenly began to move violently.

"What is it?" Zeke asked.

"I'm not sure," Taylre responded. "It looks like it's a large animal. You don't think they're going to sacrifice some poor animal on that stone table do you?"

"Could be," Zeke said. "At least it's better than a human sacrifice."

Just then, the bundle that struggled in Mr. Roberts' arms shifted, causing him to drop it on the ground. The bound object then kicked free of the ropes that bound its feet, stood up and ran.

It took all of Taylre's strength to hold Zeke back as he clutched and pawed at the ground. Devon needed his help.

CHAPTER 15

Things Left Unsaid

"**S**top him, you idiots!" David Vernon shouted, his face turning a bright red; the sound piercing the night air like a sharpened blade. "Must I do everything? What am I paying you for, to stand around and look fashionable in your robes? Get the little imp!"

Three hooded men clambered over the side of the moored boat and took off after Devon who was fleeing desperately. With his hands still tied behind his back, Devon found himself waddling more than running, knowing full well that his attempt at escape was futile. He stumbled over unseen roots and rocks, catching himself each time. He struggled on until he came upon an exposed root that stood out like a corpse's hand frantically trying to escape the grave. Devon stumbled and tumbled toward the ground, but before he hit, he was quickly scooped up by a dark lanky fellow who nearly tripped himself on his long, flowing robes.

Devon fought against the grip of the dark figure, but the strong arms that wrapped around his upper torso were soon joined with other arms that secured his thrashing legs. Devon was once again trapped.

Hooded men dragged Devon along side the Captain, retying his legs and sitting him with his back against an ancient tree stump. The Captain looked at Devon with a tired, defeated expression, then turned away, looking ashamed. His bruised eye and bloodied cheek testified of his own earlier battles.

David Vernon watched as the men he'd hired, goons he called them, recaptured Devon and dragged him screaming and fighting across the parched ground. He smiled to himself knowing that his plan was coming to fruition. It was only a matter of time until all the pieces of the puzzle came together, and he could return to his former life of ease and comfort. He shuffled over to Marjorie Anders who sat huddled, her knees drawn up to her chest like a child fighting against the cold. He sat down heavily next to her, grunting as he did, his knees cracking and his back sending spasms of pain from disuse and arthritis. He turned to look at Marjorie who avoided his gaze. Her thoughts were dark as she refused to look at Devon too, her great nephew, who now sat amongst the captured and who was now just another pawn in this charade she was forced to play.

"Marjorie, your glumness is not helping. The morale of the group cannot be upheld if you're sitting here brooding," the Mayor said.

"Shut up, David," Marjorie responded. "I don't need you to preach to me, not now. I can't believe I'm doing this again. I'm really beginning to question if this is really worth it."

The Mayor shot a glare at Marjorie, its intensity like sharp daggers flying through the air. "How dare you say that!" he said, the words spitting from his lips. "You've benefited from this as much as anyone. This is a gift, a privilege. If you doubt or challenge the gift, it will be removed, remember that."

Marjorie Anders turned her back to the Mayor, remaining silent, her arms still wrapped snuggly around her knees, but her eyes shifted involuntarily toward Devon; inside her heart began to ache.

* * * * *

10:20 pm; air is beginning to chill; behind the hills to the north a full moon is rising.

Looking down from the crest of the hill that overlooked the thick grove of trees, the flickering campfire, and the recapture of Devon, Taylre retained her tight grip on Zeke's collar keeping him firmly in place on the rough, thirsty ground. As the events below seemed to relax into a quiet interval, Zeke began to ease his own tension, his rigid fists slackening and the muscles in his back loosening. Taylre could feel the tension seeping away from Zeke as she too loosened her grip on Zeke's collar, and then finally released it altogether.

"We've got to go," Taylre whispered softly into Zeke's ear.

"Go? Now? No, we can't go. Devon's still down there," Zeke responded angrily.

"I know. But we can't do this on our own. We've got to get help," Taylre coaxed.

"There's no help, Taylre. Everyone who's supposedly got any authority in this town is down there. Even the police can't help us 'cause they're all apart of this thing too."

"Then we've got to tell your dad. He'll know what to do, or at least try to figure something out."

Zeke nodded. He knew Taylre was right. The only person who could help now was his father, though Zeke recognized that lately his father had been preoccupied and very distant to the family. But none of that mattered now. Devon's life was at stake, and for that matter, so was the Captain's. Although his father had said some harsh things about the Captain, it was obvious that Percy Proper was wrong about him. In fact there were things going on in Alder Cove that Zeke's father knew absolutely nothing about. Zeke's struggle, though, was leaving

Devon behind. He couldn't stand the thought of something happening to Devon and he not being there to help. If that occurred he would surely blame himself; a burden he felt he could not bear. But Zeke struggled with other conflicting thoughts as well: on one hand, he realized that to stay and try to fight against the dark figures below, if and when they decided to do more harm to Devon, would be useless. He was too weak and would only end up in the same predicament as both the Captain and Devon. On the other hand, Taylre would need him, and he would need her for support on the dark ride home. They'd seen too many sinister things of late, and a bicycle ride through the night filled streets of Alder Cove *alone* was just not a good idea right now. And so, the decision was made. Devon would have to wait. Zeke hoped and prayed silently that all would be well until they returned.

As if they were one body, Zeke and Taylre edged themselves back, scuffing along the dirt and grass until they were far enough away so that they could stand without being seen. They rose quietly to their feet, their legs numb and tingly from crouching in the same position too long. They walked at first, working the circulation back into their limbs, but soon found themselves running at full speed toward the fence, the gate and their waiting bikes; their feet kicking up dust and gravel as they ran.

Taylre reached the locked gate first, her long strides setting an exhausting pace. Zeke soon caught up to her just as she began leaning into the barred gate with her left shoulder, securing a small opening between the gate and the fence.

"Squeeze through, Zeke," she grunted, as beads of sweat slid down her forehead, washed over her eyebrows and splashed into her eyes causing them to sting.

Zeke stooped low under the thick chain that held the gate fast and pushed his right shoulder through the small opening, followed by his right leg and then finally his head. He then held tightly to the gate, propped his leg forcibly against the fence and pushed, giving Taylre as much of an opening as he could possibly give her. Taylre's skinny frame slid easily past the gate. When she was through, the two cousins mounted their bikes and raced off quickly toward the dimly lit town.

* * * * *

The temperature in Alder Cove had dropped drastically, and fog was starting to move in. As Zeke and Taylre rode through the barren streets, the overhead lights casting ominous shadows across the asphalt, Zeke was reminded of a horror movie he had seen recently where a group of teenagers found themselves walking through a graveyard on Halloween night. The houses to the left and right were shrouded in a light mist and stood like tombstones, their dark facades hiding ghoulish entities waiting behind the shaded windows, anticipating an attack. Zeke tried to concentrate on the road before him, knowing, subconsciously, that behind each drawn curtain or shuttered window there was a frightened and confused citizen who was too terrified to leave their home.

The two cousins crested a small hill and turned sharp on Pike Street. Taylre's house remained dark and foreboding, but Zeke's house had its porch light on, its glow casting a welcome warmth. They pulled up on the front lawn and quickly abandoned their bikes. Zeke climbed the steps two at a time and entered the house, relishing the safety and comfort of home.

Upstairs, in Devon's room, Vivian Proper sat on the hardwood floor, mascara lined her cheeks as tears continued to well up in her eyes. In her lap she held the head of Rufus, caressing his ears and body, whispering gently to him. His eyelids were half mast, his breathing ragged. When the front door opened below, Rufus raised his head slightly, but the effort seemed to be too much and he lowered it again into Vivian Proper's lap. She shifted too, her gaze turning toward the open door.

"Is anybody here!" Zeke shouted from below.

"I'm up here!" she responded, a sigh of relief escaping her lips.

Zeke bounded up the steps, again two at a time. When he reached the top with Taylre just a step behind him and entered Devon's room, Vivian Proper remained seated but held out her arms and began to cry, her tears raining down her cheeks like a deluge.

"Where have you been?" she sobbed.

Zeke leaned down and found himself enveloped in her arms with Rufus squished between them. "Where's dad?" he asked frantically.

"He's out looking for you. We came up here an hour ago wondering why it was so quiet and found you'd all snuck out the window. And," she added, "there's something wrong with Rufus. I think he's sick."

Zeke looked down at Rufus, a worried expression drifting across his face. *What did they do?* Zeke thought. *Surely Rufus tried to protect Devon. They must have done something to him to get to Devon.*

Downstairs, the front door swung open and banged loudly against the wall. There was a few moments of silence before the door was slammed shut and the sound of noisy steps were heard coming up the stairs. A few moments later, Percy Proper stood in the door frame, his hair disheveled, his glasses slightly tipped to the edge of his nose and his face expressing a myriad of emotions. At first Zeke detected the anger, the same anger he saw just the day before when Percy Proper had come to pick them up out in front of the Captain's restaurant. Next he perceived worry, a normal reaction of a loving parent who feels the suspected loss of a child. And finally, fear; a deeply etched dread that moved beyond the loss of a family member and drifted toward self preservation and survival.

Percy ran his fingers through his hair and stared down at the small group of onlookers. His face was pale and his breathing was heavy, as if he'd run a race against the devil himself. "I've been looking for you," he panted. Then, looking around the room said, "Where's Devon?"

Zeke and Taylre simply stared. They both realized that telling him about the things they'd seen would be harder than they thought.

"Where is he!" he demanded, his voice raised to a deep guttural shout.

"He's...he's" Zeke stammered. "He's at the...the river. They've taken him!" Zeke cried as tears began to spring freely from his eyes.

Percy Proper was down on his knees quickly, facing Zeke and grabbing hold of the front of his shirt, shaking him slightly. "Who's taken him?" he said, pleading for an answer.

Zeke stared up into his father's eyes, his own eyes widening. He had never seen his father like this before, and it scared him. His throat seemed to close on him and he struggled to get out the words he wanted to say. Then finally, choking past the tears and the knot that seemed to be building in his chest, he blurted out, "The mayor...and Mr. Roberts. They've taken him to the river!"

Percy Proper immediately let go of Zeke as if he'd been shocked by some unseen electrical source. Taylre and Vivian

Proper looked on in confusion, the perplexity of the situation numbing their minds. Percy slowly stood, looking around the room but not really seeing it. Then he brought his hands to his face, knocking his glasses off, and began to sob uncontrollably. "My fault," he managed to utter between short gasps. "This is all my fault. We should have never come. We should have never come to this God forsaken place."

Vivian Proper placed the now recovering Rufus into the arms of Zeke and stood up. She walked slowly and hesitantly toward her husband who seemed to be on the verge of a breakdown. "What's all your fault?" she whispered, hoping her own soft voice would bring some order to the confusion that weighted the air like heavy fog.

* * * * *

The family settled themselves uncomfortably on the couch and loveseat in the living room. Zeke was especially unsettled as he was eager to put together a rescue plan and swarm to the river like a heroic band of white knights in shining armor. However, Percy Proper was adamant that they try to remain calm and sort out the situation before attempting anything foolish.

Rufus managed to walk on his own down the stairs to join the family, though his movements were slow and uneven, nevertheless, he seemed to be recovering from the tranquilizer's potent affects.

Percy sighed heavily before beginning his tale. His face took on the appearance of a man during his last confession before a priest. "I brought you to Alder Cove," he said slowly, choosing each of his words carefully, "under false pretenses. In other words, I lied." This comment brought on looks of puzzlement from the three listeners.

"There's…" he began again. "There's something about this town that you need to know. Something that I've kept hidden from you…all of you," he said, looking guiltily into his wife's eyes.

"Many years ago some relatives of mine uncovered some secrets near the river. There was a book that was hidden in a rock, an altar really, that contained information about ways to make this area flourish and in the process make them all rich and comfortable for the rest of their lives. The book was very old, older than you can imagine, and it had been kept preserved by something…I don't know…magic, maybe? Whatever it was, the pages were all intact and had words written in some ancient language. My relatives looked around and found some professor at a college who could translate the language. From the translation they discovered everything they needed to do to bring about the promised wealth.

"Now, I need to clarify, these relatives of mine weren't the sharpest tools in the shed and they made a lot of mistakes in the process of gaining their wealth and independence. But in the end they figured it out, and what they discovered proved to be a costly.

"You see, what they discovered is that in order to have all this comfort, they needed to pay a price, every thirty years, almost like being on a payment plan. And right now, that payment is due. If it's not paid, and soon, this town and the people in it are going to pay an even heftier price, one that I am not willing to see, and trust me, neither are any of you. And so," he hesitated, breathing deeply to gain courage, " I've come here to be that payment. I am willingly giving myself up as the sacrifice."

Both Zeke and Taylre openly gasped at Percy Proper's words, bringing their hands to their mouths in an attempt to hold in the utter dismay they felt. Vivian Proper just stared. "*What* are you talking about?" she said. "Magic? Secret books? Are you crazy? What has all this got to do with Devon?"

"I'm not crazy," Percy answered calmly. "And what this has to do with Devon? Well, I'm not sure. I can't tell you why they've taken Devon. That part doesn't make sense. Unless," he mused, rubbing the sides of his unshaven face, "they've taken Devon to try to lure me. But that doesn't even make sense. I told them I would do it, why go to these extremes to get me there?" he said, as if he were talking to himself and the others were no longer in the room listening.

"This is ridiculous," Vivian Proper hissed, her face turning red with anger. "How *dare* you bring us here, your own family, just so you can prove some kind of loyalty or honor to some long forgotten curse by allowing yourself to be killed. Do you *really* think that makes you a better man? A better husband?" She suddenly stood up and moved quickly toward the front door, grabbing a set of car keys that lay on the fireplace mantle as she past. "I'm going out there to get Devon and put an end to all this nonsense."

"Stop!" Percy shouted, jumping from the couch and forcing himself between his wife and the front door. "You have no idea what these people are capable of. You have no idea *what* you're dealing with." He looked beyond her shoulder at Zeke and Taylre who still stood transfixed, unable to believe what they were hearing.

"The monster...the Korrigan at the river, it's real. As real as I am. And believe me, it is capable of some pretty ugly things," he said.

"But you said..." Taylre stammered.

"I know what I said," Percy retorted. "I was trying to protect you. I thought that if you found out about this mess that you'd all become too mixed up in it, and, well, it looks like you have...I'm so sorry." As he said this he looked at his wife, but her infuriated glare prevented him from keeping his eyes on hers. He bowed his head in shame.

Zeke managed to shake himself out of his confusion. He rose authoritatively from the couch and stood, shoulders squared and face and eyes fixed on his father. "There's got to be something we can do. I, for one, am not just going to sit here and let this happen."

"There's nothing we can do," his father said. "This curse is as ancient as time. If there were a way to fight it someone would have thought of it by now."

"Then we've just got to be smarter than everyone else. We've got to..." and then he stopped abruptly. He reached into his back pocket and retrieved a folded piece of paper which he laid out on the coffee table. Using his finger as a guide, he traced down the list he, Devon and Taylre had made earlier. Finally he came to the one he wanted and tapped the page with his finger. "Here," he said, beckoning his father to come look at the page. In bold letters Zeke had written:

6. **Stones mentioned in Devon's dream and also mentioned as part of ceremony - nothing mentioned about stones in Captain's book.**

"Stones?" his father questioned. "What's this about stones? And what dreams?"

Both Zeke and Taylre began to relate everything they'd discovered, going down the list one item at a time, telling them all that the Captain had related to the trio, and finally telling them about the dreams, the dreams Devon had seen concerning the Korrigan itself, and the dream about the lone fisherman - his statement about the stones, his calm demeanor, his graying beard and hair, and his piercing green eyes.

Both Percy and Vivian Proper listened intently, but it was not until Zeke mentioned the eyes of the dream sailor that Percy Proper reacted, sitting upright, a look of understanding showing on his face. "That's my dad," he said. "My dad visited Devon in his dream." And he smiled, the first in a very long time.

Percy lingered for just a moment in the memory of his father. He remembered his kind demeanor and the way he loved his family. But then he sobered at the thought of his father's death, knowing that his father had made the sacrifice he was about to make, yet remembering too that his father had become thoughtful and distant during the days preceding his "disappearance". At the time, when Percy was just a pimply faced fourteen year old, he thought that John Proper had indeed been lost at sea and that the stories of his falling overboard were true. It was not until he befriended Captain Bartholomew Gunner, his father's friend and business partner, that the truth was revealed: John Proper had been taken; his death was just another debt owed to the beast. Later, this revelation bothered Percy. He tried to seek answers on his own, although Bartholomew fervently discouraged him from doing so, but his curiosity got the better of him and he became too involved with the "Brotherhood". Along with his discoveries about the Korrigan and the ceremonies surrounding its existence, Percy had a falling out with Bartholomew Gunner. They no longer spoke, Percy's hatred toward him became irrational and certain.

Yet now, as Percy pondered the events of the past, knowing that a willing sacrifice was necessary, because the prophecy stated as much, why did his father need to be forcefully taken from the fishing boat one dark night? Why didn't they just wait for him to show up at the appointed time? Then, almost as if a bright light were turned on in the room, Percy realized the answer: John Proper had discovered the way to stop the curse; to finally put an end to the killing for good.

"Zeke," he said, pulling himself forcefully out of his reverie. "Do you remember the box I gave you for your birthday? The nice polished one with the key hole?"

"Yes," Zeke answered questioningly. " I have it upstairs in my room. Why?"

"Go and get it. I have a hunch that Grandpa John may have left us a clue."

CHAPTER 16

Perspectives

Zeke entered his darkened room. The curtains had been drawn and the only light that penetrated the shadows was from Zeke's digital clock that sat on his nightstand, its blue glow casting an ominous hue. Zeke glanced quickly at the numbers and noted the time to be 12:15 am, and, for some reason, perhaps it was the homey feel of the blue light cast by the neon light of the clock, he wondered about Devon and the Captain. Were they still okay? Had they been injured, or worse, tortured? But he realized that lingering on these thoughts was useless. He shook past the gruesome images that surrounded his mind and began rummaging underneath the bed for his box. He pushed aside an old train set and some books that he had placed around the box to conceal its location. Sliding it out from its hiding place, Zeke stood, holding the crafted wooden container in his arms, reverently, almost as if he were holding a squirming baby and fearing that he might drop it. He thought about removing its current contents, but then realized that time was working against them; the quicker his father had the box, the quicker they could form a plan to rescue Devon and the Captain.

Vivian Proper, Taylre and Zeke's father were waiting at the bottom of the stairs when Zeke emerged from his room. Percy Proper held out his arms to receive the box as Zeke descended. He fumbled with it momentarily, examining the polished surface and smiling at the inscription that Zeke had burned into the top. Using the small silver skeleton key that Zeke handed him, he opened the lid. A sudden whiff of stale, cheap perfume escaped from the box as the cover was raised. Zeke blushed slightly, reaching in quickly and removing a folded letter Cindy, his "girlfriend" from Halifax had given him. The paper had been drenched in perfume when he received it almost a year ago. Now, just the remaining aroma of *Jean Nate'* filled the air. Taylre looked briefly at Zeke giving him a knowing grin. Zeke was sure she'd use this information later as a way to tease him.

Other less important knick-knacks were emptied from the inside of the box, all of them items that Zeke deemed as keepsakes: a strip of black and white photos taken in a photo booth at last year's county fair depicting Zeke and Cindy sitting close, their arms wrapped around each others' shoulders, a *Swiss Army* pocket knife with Zeke's name inscribed on the outside, a polished piece of petrified wood and an amber fossil with a completely intact prehistoric insect nestled inside. The items were placed gently on the lowest stair step. Percy Proper crouched next to the items as he examined the box carefully. "Have you ever noticed anything odd about this box, Zeke?" his father asked.

"No, nothing. Just how nicely polished it was and the smooth green felt lining it has on the inside. Why should there be anything unusual about it? Didn't it just come from a regular store?"

"No," Percy answered simply, continuing to focus his attention on the box, smoothing his hands along the outside as if he were looking for an inconspicuous flaw. "This box was given to me by my dad, your grandpa, the day before he died. He made it in his woodshop out in back of the house. He told me then to keep it close, that it was his gift to the family and I was to be the keeper. I just figured it was one of those pass-along-things. You know, like the family heirloom that gets passed down from father to son and so on.

"But then there was something you said earlier when you mentioned Devon's dream. Something about stones and that got me thinking about this box. I'm not sure what the connection is, but it's got to be something."

Percy Proper continued to examine the box, running his fingers over every niche, picking lightly at any raised section and occasionally shaking it like a wrapped Christmas present. Finally he placed it on his lap and just stared at it while Zeke, Taylre and Vivian Proper looked on.

Suddenly, Percy narrowed his eyes, the crease above his brow becoming more distinct. He tilted his head sideways and stared at the box more intently. "That's funny," he said, lifting the box and holding it in front of his face. "The bottom of the box seems like it should hold more than it does."

He opened the box again and ran his finger around the inside, trying to lift the edges. Then, instead of lifting, Percy Proper pushed down on the inside of the box and the base moved slightly, as if it were balanced on a spring. A small click accompanied the movement. As he released the tension, the felt lined foundation lifted, revealing a false bottom. He raised this second lid and found, tightly packed underneath, twenty-four polished white stones, their surfaces etched in gold, each depicting a distinctive rune.

* * * * *

Peter Roberts stood like a sentry in front of the now dozing Bartholomew Gunner, and the restless, squirming Devon Proper. But he ignored the disquieting snores of the Captain and only glared occasionally at Devon, refusing to give in to his requests to use the bathroom.

He smoothed down the front of his black suit with the palm of his hand, taking pleasure in the feel of the silk material; material that was tailored exactly to his specifications, costing him well over a thousand dollars. The suit made him feel important, that his role as Guardian and Keeper of the River exalted him to the position of Peter from the New Testament who kept watch at the Pearly Gates of Heaven. However, Peter Robert's gate was not inlaid with polished pearls; his gate was charcoal black and the thing that waited inside was certainly not a heavenly being.

Standing next to the river, Roberts had a perfect view downstream for the guest he was expecting to show up any minute now. If he turned his head to the right he was also able to glance at the small group huddled around the campfire where the Mayor, Marjorie Anders, Police Chief Teddy Walford and the three "thugs": Bill, Eddy and Jeff, sat keeping themselves warm. He refused to learn the last names of the three hirelings, feeling that they were beneath him and certainly not worth remembering. *Besides*, he thought, *they won't be with us for long. There's too many secrets here. These common thieves will never keep their mouths shut.* From his location, Roberts could also see the altar, the stone edifice upon which the sacrifice would take place. On top of the altar lay the Mayor's polished box containing the twenty-four Elder Futhark Runes, the black stones with the curious markings. These stones held the power of divination, the power to summon the spirit in the Selection Ceremony and the power to call forth the Korrigan herself. Soon, the time would come when the black stones would be used to beckon the beast from the water and take its prey. When it was finally fed, at the appointed hour, it would depart, leaving behind the promise of wealth, power and comfort.

However Roberts, usually a patient man, found it difficult to wait. He shuffled his feet back and forth, digging the toe of his shoe into the soft dirt like an anxious teenager waiting for his first date. He glanced toward Devon and noticed that the boy was looking at him, a knowing grin smeared across his face. Roberts narrowed his eyes at him, thinking: *That boy knows things, I don't know how, but he does.* Then he turned again to look at the group by the fire. Catching the eye of

David Vernon, Roberts beckoned him over with the slight wave of his hand. The Mayor rose and waddled over, the black robe he wore hanging down like a tent, making the Mayor look fatter than he already was.

"What time is it? Peter Roberts inquired.

"It's ten minutes later than the last time you asked. Why? are you nervous about something?" Responded the Mayor.

"Nervous? No," Roberts retorted, scuffing his toe further into the dirt. "I'm just anxious to see this come to an end. You know how I hate to see things unravel. I like all my ducks in a row, if you know what I mean. Take that boy for instance, the one they found in the back yard of that man's house. He could potentially cause us all sorts of trouble: spouting his mouth off, telling people what he'd seen, here, by the river."

"Nonsense," the Mayor responded. "Police Chief Walford has seen to that. The boy was found to have had too many 'drugs' in his system. Everyone's convinced that whatever the boy was sniffing was also doing the talking...*if* you know what *I* mean. And, as far as the other boy is concerned...well, let's just say he got a little too close to the water during snack time. She can't be expected to starve while she waits for the appointed hour, now can she? And so, the 'snack' is now considered a runaway - whereabouts unknown." David Vernon laughed, then looked over his shoulder at the dark water near the stand of trees. Then he added, "Perhaps next time the young man from the backyard will pay attention to signs rather than ignore them."

"And Proper?" Roberts questioned. "Shouldn't he have arrived by now?"

"Relax," David Vernon said, slapping Roberts lightly on the shoulder. "He'll be here. He knows the appointed time, and

Marjorie assures me he won't be late. You just keep your eye on the river and give the signal when he arrives."

The Mayor began to walk back to the warmth of the fire when Roberts said, "David." Mayor Vernon turned, an unpleasant flicker from the fire gleaming from the corner of his eye. "Simon Peter once said, 'whereby are given unto us exceeding great and precious *promises*: that ye might be partakers of the divine nature'. Remember what *you* promised me."

David Vernon smiled weakly. "Of course, Peter. You know my word is good."

"It better be," Roberts answered. Then, when the Mayor was out of earshot, Roberts whispered, "For your sake, it better be."

*   *   *   *   *

1:12 am; light fog settling in the bay; a full moon reflecting against the water.

Percy Proper had been given a key when he first arrived in Alder Cove from Marjorie Anders. The meeting was brief and very awkward. He was told simply that the key would allow him access to the marina and that a small fishing boat would be waiting for him at berth number 8. As he pulled into the parking lot next to the marina's gate, he felt a chill of trepidation course down his spine. He turned off the car's engine and sat silently, listening to the click and clatter of the cooling engine. He reached up and adjusted the rearview mirror so that he could see himself in its reflection. Taking off his glasses he examined the dark circles around his eyes and noted with a sigh how bloodshot they were. *This is crazy* he thought. *Why did I ever let myself get caught up in this mess? And now, to make things worse, I've enlisted two fourteen year olds to try and persuade a bunch of over zealous "brotherhood members" to stop their foolishness and let everybody go home.* He laughed out loud at this thought. *Right, let everybody go home. Like that'll ever happen.*

He exited the car and, because it was his habit to do so, locked the door. He carried with him a small backpack containing the polished box Zeke had hidden so dutifully under his bed. He walked slowly to the gate, like a man who carried a great weight on his shoulders. Much heavier than the small pack he now held.

The key slipped easily into the lock and with only minimal effort, it turned, allowing the gate to swing open. As he slipped through the gate, his thoughts went out to his wife who had elected to stay home, nursing the still ailing Rufus, and mollifying the anger she still felt over her husband's betrayal. *Make this right,* he remembered her saying as he walked out the door. *Bring my children back safely, make those people pay for what they've done, and make...it...right.* She had closed the door then, bowing her head as she did so to hide the tears that filled her eyes. He stood for just a moment on the front porch, then turned with determination, vowing in his heart that he would indeed make it right.

Now, as he walked the uneven docks toward berth number 8, Percy Proper tried to hold on to that determination, but his grasp was weak, and fear kept tugging at him.

*   *   *   *   *

To Zeke, the ride through the darkened town over the dirt road and up to the fence that kept out unwanted visitors was like déjà vu. To Taylre, it was more like a reoccurring nightmare, one that she would just as soon forget.

The cousins parked their bikes in the same manner as before, against the barbed wire-topped fence. Zeke stared at the gate, realizing just how much he hated the process of squeezing through the small opening. Just thinking about it made the sides of his head hurt. But enter he must. Devon, the Captain and his dad were counting on him, another painful squeeze on the side of his head was the least he could do.

Zeke approached the gate first, grasping the metal frame tightly and pulling back to allow Taylre enough room to squeeze through. Taylre confidently strolled up to the gate and removed a small backpack from her shoulders. She unzipped the pack and produced a set of bolt cutters.

"Wha…" Zeke started to say.

"Your dad gave them to me before we left," Taylre said, reading Zeke's surprised expression. "He got them out of his tool chest in the garage. Pretty cool, uh?"

"Yeah, pretty cool," Zeke responded, a look of amazement still inscribed across his face.

She applied the end of the scissor like cutters up to the thick chain and began to clamp down on the handles, but to no effect. She readjusted her grip and tried again as Zeke looked on with some amusement at her struggle. She grunted this time, putting all of her weight into trying to close the handles and break the thick link, but again her effort was not rewarded; the chain remained firm with only a small dent in the metal to show for her attempt. Zeke reached up impatiently and took the cutters from her. "Here, let me try," he exclaimed." Then he too grunted with an extraordinary effort to try and break the chain, and managed only to put a little deeper dent into the metal. This time Taylre grabbed onto the handle with Zeke. "Let's do this together," she said. "I think we'll get more accomplished if we work side by side rather than as individuals."

Zeke looked at her and knew that she meant more than just trying to break a chain. There was something beyond the gate that needed to be broken as well; Zeke knew that he was foolish to think that he could do it on his own. "You're right," he said, nodding slightly and smiling up at Taylre. "Let's do this."

Then, with a mighty effort on both of their parts, they pushed, pulled and squeezed the handles, watching the blade slowly cut through the metal until finally the link snapped in half, the heavy chain and lock falling harmlessly to the ground.

With the chain broken, the gate swung open freely. Taylre and Zeke picked up their bikes from the ground and rode through the opening aiming toward the same small hill from which they initially observed Devon's capture. But this time, they were prepared, or, at least, hoped they were.

* * * * *

Devon was getting cold and the ropes that held his hands firmly behind his back were cutting off the circulation. As he struggled to keep himself warm, he could feel an uncomfortable tingly sensation that always accompanied the loss of blood flow in a limb, something his mom always referred to as having your hand fall asleep. He tried kicking his legs out in front of him, but the task was made more difficult because of the ropes that also bound his feet. Eventually he found that if he just kept his legs slightly bent at the knees and leaned into the old stump he was propped up against, he would be able to stay at least relatively comfortable. The cold, however, was inevitable, and he envied those cloaked figures who sat by the small fire.

Beside him, the Captain continued to snore, and when Devon looked at him, he felt a pang of sympathy, but at the same time, an ache of frustration. He understood the Captain's predicament and felt bad for the beating he obviously received at the hands of Mr. Roberts and the other three thugs. However, Devon also felt that the Captain could at least wake up so that they could work out a way to get out of the mess they were in.

"Hey," Devon whispered sharply, looking around at the others, making sure that Roberts hadn't heard. Because of all the people that Devon had encountered tonight, he feared Roberts the most. Roberts had a way of unsettling Devon. When Roberts stared at him, he felt a chill hit his body, as if someone had left a window open during a winter storm. It was a cool draft that made his skin squirm and his thoughts go fuzzy. Devon also felt something else when he looked at Roberts, and that confused him, mostly because he couldn't help but feel that what he saw in Roberts' eyes was fear. Fear of him.

Devon leaned over as far as he could, balancing himself precariously on his right butt cheek, and threw his legs out, kicking the Captain on the bottom of his left foot, while at the same time hissing, " Captain," as loudly as he could without drawing attention to himself.

The Captain stirred uneasily and lifted a swollen eyelid to look at Devon. He smiled weakly and then struggled into a sitting position. The right side of the Captain's face had a large bruise that covered his cheek. The left side had an abrasion where clotted, dried blood hung in wax-like drips with tiny bits of dirt and rock clinging to them. He shook his head lightly, trying to wake himself, then softly cleared his throat. "Quite a day we're havin' huh, lad?"

"Captain," Devon urged, again using his sharp whispery voice. "We've got to do something. We can't just sit here."

"Well, boy," the Captain said, mimicking Devon's whispered voice. "There's not much we can do all tied up like we are. Looks like we're just going to have to wait this one out and see what happens. What time is it, do ya think?"

"I overheard Mr. Roberts talking to that big man over there, saying it was just after one o'clock in the morning."

"Well, it's getting close then. The witchin' hour is two o'clock. That's when their little ritual will start. That's what they're all waitin for." The Captain tried to move into a more comfortable position and groaned inwardly. The stiffness in his arms and legs were sending sharp jolts of pain through his body.

Devon watched the Captain labor in his rigid movements and again felt that pang of sympathy. "What happened, Captain? How did you end up here?"

Finally settled, the Captain turned his head to look at Devon, a heavy weight of frustration showing itself across his features. "Roberts," he whispered harshly. " He met me just down stream a bit," and he shifted his gaze slightly to the right to indicate the direction.

"I should have expected him, but I got too caught up in my own thinking. I got soft for just a moment. Probably a good thing too. Folks who be apt to get too close to...well...you know...the thing in the water there," and he moved his head to indicate the dark water under the stand of trees, " tend to get themselves eaten. It gives me the shivers just thinking about it. It's like I can feel the thing watching us right now."

Devon nodded slowly. He could feel the presence of something big and evil very close, and it caused the hairs on the back of his neck to stand on end.

The Captain continued his tale. "Then, before I knew it, there were others all around my boat. They tipped it over before I even had a chance to grab my gun or my knife. Next thing I know I'm up on shore with two or three of them beatin down on me with their fists and kickin' me with their big boots. I went black after that and then woke up to find you sittin' here."

"But why? Why did you come?" Devon asked.

"Why? Well, to do what I should have done years ago...stop them." Again he indicated with the shift of his gaze and a jutting movement of his chin toward the small group by the fire.

"I've always known what they were up to, but I never did anything to stop them. I guess I thought if I just left it alone it would somehow go away, but deep inside I knew...I knew that I had to do something. But I was too much of a coward...until today that is. Today, I decided to come out here and set things straight." Then the Captain chuckled to himself, a sad sort of laughter that has no happiness in its sound. "And look where it's gotten me...all tied up, beaten and bloodied."

"But at least you tried, Captain," Devon said, trying his best to give a reassuring smile. The Captain felt humbled by the fact that a twelve year old boy was trying to comfort him. Humbled, but at the same time ashamed. "What happens next?" Devon asked.

"There's some things I'm not sure of, some specific details of how the ritual goes, but eventually they take the chosen sacrifice and put it on that altar over there. Then I'm sure that either Vernon or Roberts will have some things to say to appease the beast and then...well, I'm sure you can use your imagination. I just hope we're not here to witness it. Seein' a thing like that would haunt a person for the rest of their life."

There was some sudden movement from near the fire as the three hooded men were lead quickly by Roberts past Devon and the Captain and over to the edge of the river. Both of the captives looked up at the sound of an approaching motorboat, its engine slowing to a smooth idle.

Percy Proper stood in the center of the drifting craft with an armful of rope that he tossed ashore. The rope was gathered by the dark crew along the bank and tied to a thick root that stuck out of the dry ground. They gently pulled on the rope until the boat came to rest with a light thump in the soft sand surrounding the steep shoreline. Percy Proper clamored over the side of the boat with nimble agility, climbing quickly up the side of the embankment and finding himself suddenly surrounded by the hooded figures. Roberts approached in a slow, cautious manner, his flat, humorless smile expressing confidence, but his movements shouting a sense of fear.

"Right on time," Roberts said, his lips trembling.

"Just like I said I would be," Percy Proper responded. Then, looking past Roberts toward Devon and the Captain, said, "Why are they here? Why did you bring my son into this? It was never part of the deal."

Roberts turned to look at the captives and nervously laughed. "That?" he said, turning back to face Mr. Proper. "That is complicated. Something you'll discover in due time." He then nodded slightly to the three thugs who, as if on cue, grabbed hold of Percy Proper's arms and dragged him toward the fire.

* * * * *

Taylre and Zeke looked on from the small knoll overlooking the stand of trees and the ominous black flow of the river. When Percy Proper pulled up in the small boat, Zeke glanced down at his watch: 1:45 am, his father was right on time. He pulled off the day pack from his back and carefully unzipped the top pocket. From inside, he withdrew a see- through plastic zip-lock bag, its contents clinking together like dice being thrown in a game of chance. He held the bag up to his face and felt a soft warmth begin to radiate from it along with a charged, pulsing, electrical strength.

CHAPTER 17

Stones

Marjorie Anders stood with her hands folded in front of her, her eyes downcast. The dark robe she wore, the hood pulled back revealing her tortured features, seemed to mock its wearer. She fought to keep back the tears that tried to well up in her eyes, nevertheless, the trembling lips and the shaking hands gave away far too much of her already shredded emotions. She thought about Taylre for the first time in the last couple of days and felt a spasm of guilt. She wondered what Taylre would say if she ever discovered what her grandmother was involved in.

Mr. Roberts stood next to her, too close for Marjorie's comfort, constantly gazing at his watch. He tapped it twice, and once held it up to his ear to see if it was still ticking. He shuffled his feet anxiously, and habitually ran his hands down the front of his expensive suit in an attempt to reassure himself that things were running smoothly and on time.

David Vernon stood before the now kneeling Percy Proper and spoke with a supposed air of certainty. But his authority only seemed more ridiculous because of the gold trimmed black robe that hung over him, too short at the bottom, exposing white socks with red and blue sport stripes.

"Keep a good grip on him boys. We can't afford to have the solemnity of our ritual disturbed." David Vernon said, glancing over his shoulder at the stone altar, its surface marked with faded stains of violence from years past.

"There's no need to do this, David!" Percy Proper shouted. "I've promised you my cooperation, I'm not going to take that away now."

"You say that now, Percy. But, you see, things have changed, as we thought they might, so we had to make other arrangements. When you learn about the new developments, your current level of cooperation may change. I can't take the risk of allowing you to mess things up." The Mayor then glanced curiously at the small pack that Percy Proper wore on his back.

"What have we here, Percy? Have you brought a weapon with you?" David Vernon pointed to the backpack. While the three robed thugs continued to hold on to Mr. Proper, Chief Walford obediently removed the bag and unzipped the small pouch, removing the wooden box Percy Proper's father had made, the words - **Property of Zeke Proper - Do not Disturb**, staring almost accusingly up at the Mayor. When David Vernon saw the box his eyes grew wide with fear. At first he stepped back a few paces as if the box itself held some sort of power. Then slowly, but reluctantly, he stepped forward, carefully taking the box from Walford's pudgy hands. He opened the lid warily, as if he expected something to jump out at him. When he had the top completely open, he took in a deep breath, exhaling gradually. "You had me worried, Percy. For a moment there I thought you'd brought the Antithesis, but, of course, we all know that to be just a rumor. Right, Marjorie?" he said, looking at Marjorie Anders who continued to sit next to the heat of the fire, her head bowed, her hands nervously rubbing each other.

David Vernon turned back to Percy Proper. "John, your father, was always a good story teller. Stories of white stones that would supposedly put an end to our good fortune. But I guess this tale turned out to be false, too. Just a lot of nonsense." The Mayor threw the box into the fire. Marjorie stood suddenly as ashes and sparks floated into the air. She brought her hands to her mouth in shock as she watched the polished box her brother created begin to catch fire.

Roberts nudged David Vernon and showed him his watch. The time was 1:53 am. "I know, Peter," the Mayor exclaimed, his voice suggesting a hint of annoyance. "Bring the boy."

At the mention of Devon, Percy Proper began to fight against the strong arms that held him down. "What's this all about, Vernon? Why have you brought my son here? He has nothing to do with any of this! This was never part of the deal!"

"The deal has changed, Percy. The runes were cast in the Selection Ceremony, and, unfortunately, *your* name wasn't chosen, as we had originally hoped it would be. I'm sorry, Percy, but the message was very clear. Your son, Devon, has been selected as the sacrifice."

"NO!" Percy Proper thrashed against his captors, trying in vain to pull himself free. His face was thick with sweat and his eyes were alive with the fire of anger. Then, struggling to bring his voice to a calm, reasoning level he said, "I was the willing sacrifice. I pledged myself to this ritual. You told me the legacy must be passed from father to son. I am only doing that which my own father did. I'm doing this for the town and for my family. Please, David, honor your promise. Take me and let my son go home."

David Vernon shook his head sadly. "I can't do that, Percy. The stones don't lie," he glanced toward the altar where there lay another highly polished wooden box, its lid closed tightly with the firelight gleaming off its surface. "When I raise the lid and expose the black onyx stones, the Korrigan will rise from the depths and take its victim. If it's the right one it will leave and prosperity will continue here in Alder Cove. If it rises and finds you on the altar, it will certainly take you as its meal, but it won't leave. It will descend again to the bottom of the river and wait until the right sacrifice is given. Until then its curse will reign upon this land. The drought will continue, the fish will flee the nets, and this town will die, along with you, your family and the rest of the inhabitants; there is no escape. The Korrigan's wrath will bear down on this town like never before.

"The entity that guided us during the Selection Ceremony as we cast the black stones made it very clear who the sacrifice was to be...it's not you, Percy. We knew it would be *someone* in your family. We just couldn't be certain who. So we had you come to Alder Cove and bring your family with you." The Mayor knelt down in front of Percy Proper, his eyes almost pleading, his voice a faded whisper. "But know this, Percy. You and your family *will* be rewarded. You will have riches beyond belief. Imagine it: a large house over looking the bay; fine clothing, a beautiful car, anything your heart desires. And, consider this, Percy, *you* will become my right hand man. What more could you ask for?"

As Mayor David Vernon spoke, Peter Roberts passed him on his left, dragging Devon by the collar, his arms and legs tied, his heels scraping small furrows in the dry ground. Roberts turned sharply as he heard the Mayor tell Percy Proper that he would make him his right hand man, but Roberts said nothing; the flash of anger that crossed his features, unseen by the Mayor, spoke for volumes.

"But Devon isn't a willing sacrifice," Percy Proper explained. "The prophecy in the Book clearly states that the gift *must* be willing. Devon isn't willing. He knows nothing about any of this. Do you really think Devon will give his life to the Korrigan?"

The small assemblage standing by the fire all turned to look at Roberts who, still holding onto Devon's collar, stood next to the altar. Percy Proper looked imploringly at his son. Devon stared back, a calm expression drawn across his face. He had heard the entire conversation between his father and the Mayor. His understanding of the situation was clear; his recollection of the Korrigan dream becoming a reality.

"I'm not so sure about that, Percy. Look at your son and tell me he wouldn't gladly switch places with you," the Mayor said.

Percy Proper did look, but this time it was the look of a father who had failed. He felt ashamed and humbled because what he saw in his son's eyes was the confirmation that Devon would indeed take his place. That realization deeply disturbed Percy Proper, mainly because he realized that *he* should have fought for his family with the same courage that Devon was exhibiting, but with the courage to live for his family, not to die.

"I won't let you do this, David," Percy stated, a grimace of pain showing across his face as one of the goons twisted his arm.

"There's nothing you can do, Percy. The time is at hand; the beast must be fed. And, Percy," the mayor said, bending so close that Percy Proper could smell the Mayor's putrid breath, "if you try anything I will have Officer Walford shoot you."

Percy Proper lowered his head in resignation. Things were not going according to plan. He never suspected that Devon was going to be the sacrifice, only the bait. He shifted his gaze inconspicuously toward the small knoll that lay to the south. His thoughts went out to Zeke and Taylre and hoped that they would somehow pick up on his effort at telepathy: *get help* he thought. *Don't try to be heroes. I can't bear the thought of losing two children in one night.*

* * * * *

Zeke and Taylre had both seen and heard enough. The big picture of how things really were was now very clear to them. The plan that Percy Proper had outlined to them before setting out on this adventure had been plain. But now, with Devon being the focus of a rescue along with Zeke's father, the plan had drastically changed. It would no longer be a matter of waiting for the right moment to sneak down, untie the Captain and Devon, retreat to the boat that was moored to the river bank, and then somehow hope that Percy Proper could manage his way out of his own predicament. Now, the problem was much more complex. Not only was Devon's life in danger, but Percy Proper too required assistance, as did the Captain. Zeke and Taylre certainly had their hands full. For this reason, they decided to move their location from the small hill overlooking the river, to a thistle infested meadow that directly bordered the river; just north of the stand of trees. Although the location presented a more uncomfortable staging area, their view of the proceedings was much improved. From here they could see the altar, its stone walls unobscured by the flickering firelight. They could see the small polished wooden box that lay on its end, that once held the white stones, the ones that he now carried in a sealed, clear plastic bag.

A faint warm breeze began to blow, causing some of the thorns from the thistles to brush up against Zeke's pant leg and others to snag on Taylre's t-shirt. Their current location was proving to be prickly, but as the two cousins huddled around the plastic bag containing the white stones, their sense of discomfort faded as quickly as it came. The stones, which now began to glow as well as release a positive sort of energy, seemed to possess a strength that was being passed on to both Zeke and Taylre; a strength that was increasing the closer they moved to the altar.

Zeke considered the words he overheard the Mayor speak to his father. Zeke had turned to Taylre when the Mayor had opened the lid of the box. He could have sworn that a terrified expression had past over David Vernon's face. The look on Taylre's face seemed to confirm that idea; it wasn't just the flickering light of the campfire playing tricks on them. Zeke shuddered inwardly when the Mayor threw his box in the fire, but that act itself proved that the Mayor had something to fear from the box. Zeke was sure that he now held that something; that the white stones *were* the Antithesis that the Mayor's trembling voice had spoken of.

At 1:58 am, with the bright reflection of a full moon gleaming off of the dark river water, Peter Roberts placed the bound, calm body of Devon Proper on the altar. Percy Proper watched helplessly while the three hooded men held his shoulders and arms firmly and as the cold tip of the police officer's standard issue revolver rested against the side of his head.

At 1:59 am, Mayor David Vernon shuffled his way over to take his place at the head of the altar. Marjorie Anders, pulling the hood of her robe up over her head, moved lithely, though reluctantly, to the foot of the altar. Roberts remained at the side, holding down Devon, yet the need to do so was unnecessary; Devon remained calm and still.

Roberts glanced quickly toward the Mayor and the Mayor looked up to see the cold stare that Roberts gave him. David Vernon's forehead frowned momentarily, but then Robert's expression turned to a pleasant smile; nevertheless his eyes still held onto a warning. The Mayor felt a sudden rush of unease and started to say something to Roberts when suddenly the dark water to his left began to churn, its surface boiling over slowly like thick lava.

Zeke and Taylre, still hidden among the weeds, saw the water begin to bubble and felt the faint warm breeze start to pick up, then suddenly turn cold. They were reminded of the day in the Captain's boat when the hail storm had appeared, bringing with it a chilling wind and frozen chunks of ice.

As the water churned, the twenty-four white Stones that Zeke held in the plastic bag began to glow with greater intensity. Zeke crouched lower, bending himself around the bag in an attempt to cover the stone's growing light. He feared that soon the increasing illumination would reveal their location. Taylre tried to conceal the light as well, using the now empty backpack as a shade. However, the light, it seemed, was taking on a life of its own. Zeke could feel the stones lifting, pushing upward against his body and trying to escape the plastic seal that confined them.

At the head of the altar, his back facing Zeke and Taylre's hiding place, David Vernon reached for the smooth polished box, but his hands trembled. The beast that caused the waters to churn was directly behind him, and though it was still hidden beneath the murky water, he feared its savagery, its rancid smell, the darkness that surrounded it like a thick wet blanket, and he feared the cold depthless eyes that seemed to suck the humanity from him, leaving him shaking and ill for days and months after. But the rewards, he felt, were worth it. *A life of ease and luxury*, he thought, *would always be worth it.*

As the Mayor's hand touched the box's smooth surface, preparing to lift the lid and expose the black stones that would call forth the Korrigan, Robert's hand slammed down on top of his.

"You are a deceiver, David," Roberts said, the cold stare returning to his expression. "You promised me that my place would be secure with you; that I would always be your second, but you have lied to me. I *hate* liars, David. I hate liars more than any other kind of sinner."

"Wha...what are you talking about, Peter?" The Mayor said. "We're in the middle of the Ritual here. The time is at hand. We must continue. We don't have time for this nonsense!"

"I heard you when you thought I wasn't listening. You told Proper that he would be your second in command. But you promised that to me. You lied!" Roberts said, raising his hands in front of him, his palms turned upward. "God hath said that 'all liars shall have their part in the lake which burneth with fire and brimstone'. I warned you, David. Now *you* will pay."

Robert's movements were quick. David Vernon barely had time to breath before Roberts grabbed the ropes that bound Devon's feet with his left hand and the ropes that bound his arms with his right, and flung him to the earth. When Devon hit the ground, a puff of dirt flew up around his face, causing him to cough and hack. Roberts then turned on David Vernon, seizing him by the hair on the top of his head and slamming his face into the stone altar. Blood and snot washed across the stone table while the polished wooden box slid off of the platform, its lid breaking open when it crashed to the ground, scattering the black onyx stones across the dirt.

The black stones, their exteriors smooth and glass-like, mirrored the light of the full moon that hung in the sky like a brilliant, accusing face. As the reflection glinted off the surface of the dark water, the Korrigan rose, obeying the call of the stones like a siren's plea. Its black hulk, now standing above the altar, overshadowed the light of the moon. It looked down on the scene before it, a momentary expression of confusion passing across its mottled features, its blood red eyes with their yellow piercing centers, staring at Roberts and the Mayor.

In the presence of the Korrigan, the small group of onlookers felt a sudden wash of depression, darkness, and despair flow over them. Everyone's thoughts became black, and their efforts to move away from the beast was like trying to sludge through thick, oozing mud. Officer Walford dropped his weapon and fell back in the dirt. He tried crawling away, using his elbows and heels to push himself, but his cumbersome, overweight body slowed his movements, and he failed to raise his butt off of the ground, its wide girth slowing any progress he might otherwise have made.

The three hirelings, their hoods hiding their features, let go of Percy Proper and turned. Each running in a different direction, though their legs felt thick and heavy. On their faces were the terror stricken expressions of a scream, but no sound could escape their lips.

Marjorie Anders also fell backward when the Korrigan rose. She looked up into its evil eyes for only a brief moment before she forced herself to turn away. She scrambled on her hands and knees toward Devon who lay on his side on the ground and grabbed him, pulling him in close, wrapping her arms around him in a protective manner. Devon whimpered softly in her arms and she whispered softly through her own tears, "I'm sorry. I'm sorry," over and over again.

Percy Proper continued to kneel on the ground, his mouth open in awe at the sight before him, his head shaking in wonder. Within his mind, somewhere deep in its recesses, Percy had always thought that the Korrigan perhaps wasn't real; that the stories the Captain told him about his father's death were just legends, tales meant to spark a youngster's imagination; that in fact his father had died at sea, just the way everyone said it had happened. But now, standing before him, sinister and ugly, *was* the thing of legend. The Korrigan, risen, massive, with its sharp shark-like teeth bared and its glaring, unblinking eyes, stared expressionlessly and unmercifully toward the two individuals that stood before it, poised near the altar.

David Vernon could feel the hot blood dripping from his nose and was sure that it was broken. He was dazed, his mind clouded with a thick haze. Nevertheless, he knew what Roberts had done, and his anger, assisted by the presence of the Korrigan, rose like a red blur before his eyes. He could feel Roberts' hand still gripping his hair and he reached sluggishly with his own hand to try to tear it free, but Roberts' hold on David Vernon's hair was vice-like, not because Roberts was still trying to pummel the Mayor, but because his own terror froze him.

As Roberts stared up into the face of the Korrigan, he realized, too late, that he had made a huge mistake. By casting aside the one true sacrifice, the Selected One, Roberts had inadvertently changed the course of events. The Korrigan, responding to the call of the black stones, ascended, expecting to find its meal, the one she'd been created to consume. But the Korrigan was an unintelligent eating machine; a demon with one thought only: to serve her master, *her* father, the mischievous Loki. She could not distinguish between the Selected One and just a passing meal. Its appetite would be satisfied, one way or another. Roberts had been quick when he shoved the Mayor's face into the stone of the altar, but he was no match for the speed of the Washer Woman. With hardly a moment to utter a last groan, the Korrigan snatched Roberts' by his head, its multilayered teeth snapping down on his flesh with an eerie crunch, pulling him upward. But Roberts still had his fingers entwined tightly in David Vernon's hair, and as he rose in the grip of the Korrigan, he tore the Mayor's hair from its roots.

David Vernon, his hands raised to his bleeding scalp, let out a painful scream and stumbled to the side while his feet became entangled in his robes. He fell heavily on his back in the dirt beside the altar. He rolled over awkwardly, like a turtle trapped on its shell, and tried to stand. As he pulled himself up, the flailing feet of Roberts, dangling just above the Mayor, his head still caught in the grasp of the Korrigan, kicked violently against David Vernon's shoulder. David lost his balance and fell again, this time stumbling backward, rolling down the steep bank and landing with a splash in the black water next to the immense figure of the Korrigan. Panicking, the Mayor thrashed about in the water like a drowning dog as he attempted to claw his way back to the river's edge, but his movements were slow and clumsy. Gasping, he began to swallow large amounts of water in his attempt to breathe. With nothing to grab onto and no place to set his feet, the Mayor sank, his hands reaching one last time into the empty night air. Soon he disappeared beneath the deep, dark water, his movements becoming stilled as he descended to the bottom, his final breath rising as one large bubble bursting the surface.

Roberts' final moments ended quickly, although the pain he felt was immeasurable. With incredible strength the Korrigan tossed Roberts into the air, flipping him around like a dog playing with a stick, catching him by his feet. Then, with the same deft agility, the beast plunged Roberts head first into the ground, crushing whatever life remained in him. Roberts' body was then swallowed whole, his existence wiped away, becoming nothing more than a faded memory.

The Korrigan, its ravenous appetite barely quenched, turned its attention to the remaining group of terrified observers. It eyed each of them, perhaps trying to decide which morsel to feast on first. However, behind her, still crouched in the thistles, Zeke and Taylre sat, still shielding the ever increasing intensity of light that escaped the white stones. The bag that contained them began to melt and small droplets of liquid plastic ran harmlessly through Zeke's fingers. Now exposed to the night air, the stones began to glow brilliantly. Taylre was forced to shield her eyes against the whiteness. Zeke could only close his eyes as the stones, by some unseen power of their own, lifted, pulling his hands with them upward until they shone over his head. Zeke rose from his kneeling position and stood among the tall weeds, his hiding place no longer concealed, and began to advance, being led by the stones themselves, toward the altar and the Korrigan.

Droplets of dew clinging to the weeds and grass began to soak into Zeke's pant legs as he drifted forward. He became unusually aware of the weight that the water added to his clothing, but then realized that he was aware of many things at this moment: The fresh salt air, the scent of pine from the distant forests in the hills beyond, the smell of flowers he had no name for, grass, the colors of the night, the clear brightness of the stars above. To Zeke, it seemed that his natural senses had become intensified ten or twenty times their normal capacity. His thoughts, too, were clear, and he knew from some inward instinct that the white stones he held were the reason why.

Hold the stones high, let their light shine and live.

His legs felt light and powerful. His breathing became deep and clear. He felt as if he could leap over the highest tree or run through the fields at incredible speeds. The strength he felt as he extended his arms over his head with the twenty four stones cradled in his hands enabled him with this power. He felt clean and pure.

Hold the stones high, let their light shine and live.

The black stones that lay scattered on the ground beside the altar suddenly began to lose their luster. The etchings, the marks of some ancient language, faded as if they were being sucked back into the stones themselves. Smoke rose from their surfaces as the stones began to melt, as if the very ground around them were becoming super-heated, drawing them back into the earth from whence they came.

The Korrigan, sensing the destruction of the black stones, turned from the victims before her and stared, terror-stricken, at the blazing bright light of the white stones, their approach coming closer and closer. The mouth of the Korrigan fell open and from its terrified lips, it uttered a scream that all of the witnesses would never forget for the rest of their lives - the scream of a thousand agonizing deaths. With the scream there came an odor so foul that the scattered survivors began to retch and vomit across the dusty earth.

Suddenly, flies, black as night, appeared from nowhere, buzzing and swarming around the Korrigan. Their energy, as they spun around the beast, seemed to lift it from the water and then set it down heavily on the ground, knocking over the stones that made up the altar. Then the Korrigan, its howl of death ended, plodded its way toward Zeke and the stones. It seemed to sense its own impending doom and so, as if by some deep survival instinct, attempted one last try at fighting its enemy. Ineffectually shading its eyes against the brightness of the stones, the Korrigan advanced on Zeke. The terror in its face was rising; another scream building.

Zeke stood his ground. The very air around him seemed to be charged with electricity. The body hairs covering both Zeke and Taylre began to stand on end.

Dark, oozing blood began to flow forth from the eyes of the Korrigan. Its sharpened razor-like teeth began to chatter. Its mottled skin began to shake and tremble as if the beast were about to erupt into a violent seizure.

And then a light.

A single intense beam of light, brighter than the sun on a brilliant summer day, shone forth, aimed directly at the eyes of the Korrigan. Zeke was pushed backward, his strength fading to that of a crippled old man, as if the stones themselves were drawing upon his purity, his vitality and his youth. He landed with a thud upon the ground, but managed to keep his arms raised above his head, hearing and obeying a still small voice, the echo of a distant declaration: *Hold the stones high, let their light shine and live.*

The light penetrated the eyes and mouth of the Korrigan. It burned with a brilliant heat, tearing away the flesh from the beast. Smoke and ash lifted and caught on the cool night wind, scattering amongst the dark water of the river and among the parched remains of dried weeds and grass that edged its banks.

The beast tried to scream again, but the sound was buried beneath the rushing hurricane of light that enveloped, and eventually erased, the blackness. Then finally, the beast, the Washer-Woman, the Korrigan, what was left of it, fell back into the deep water, slipping lifelessly into the slow, steady stream; a carcass of rotted, burnt flesh becoming food for the fish.

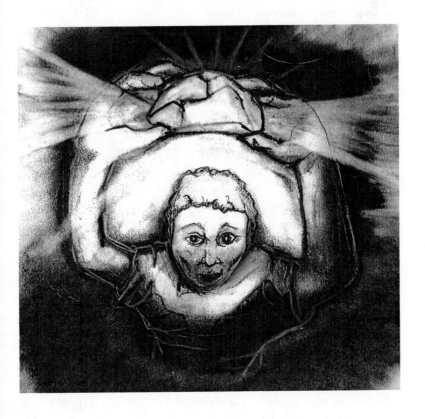

CHAPTER 18

Promises

At first there was only darkness, then, slowly, though the effort was painful, Zeke opened his eyes. He became aware of the hard ground beneath his back and realized he was lying flat on the dirt. Directly above him, Zeke could see the gentle flutter of leaves as a cool, early morning wind passed through the trees to his right. The sky was gray with a touch of muffled light that announced the coming of a new day, but it struggled to break the precipice of the horizon. His head ached. He tried to raise his arms to bring his hands to his temples to rub away some of the pain, but lifting was difficult. His arms felt like dead weights, as if he'd been lifting heavy objects over and over until his limbs remained exhausted, spent, like the rest of his body.

To his right, Zeke heard a quick shuffling movement and he turned his head instinctually to see what had made the noise, but as he did so a sharp current of pain shot up from his lower back through his neck and ended abruptly in the middle of his forehead. He squeezed his eyes shut again and waited for the sensation to pass. After a few moments, the pain subsided, though an echo of tenderness still lingered. He realized his movements, at least for a little while, had to be smooth and slow. Gritting his teeth, readying himself for another jolt of pain, Zeke began to gently slide his right leg upward, dragging his foot across the dry earth, until his knee was positioned above him, his right foot flat on the ground. So far so good. He took in a deep breath and slowly brought up his other leg, his knees now resting against each other. His arms came next as he placed his hands flat on the ground and worked himself up on his elbows, raising his head slightly off of the ground at the same time. Lifting his head caused a wave of nausea to wash over him, but it too quickly subsided and he had, for the first time, a glimpse of his surroundings.

Zeke looked first to his right where he had first heard the shuffling sound, like the heel of a boot scraping across cement. There, sitting with her back up against what used to be the stone altar, was Taylre, her knees drawn up with her arms wrapped tightly around them. Her head was bowed low and she was sobbing quietly, occasionally sniffing back her tears, the cause of the shuffling sound Zeke had heard. Her knees were scuffed and dirty. Her hair was matted; the once tight curls now hanging down the sides of her face in loose tangles.

Zeke shifted his gaze momentarily from Taylre to scan the area. What he saw made him gasp inwardly. The surrounding vicinity looked like a battle scene. Broken pieces of the stone altar were strewn about the dirt. A heavy, thick, smoky mist settled on the ground like fog blown in from the sea. Bits of charred grass simmered from the earth and the sides of many of the trees in the small wooded area had burnt bark that still showed signs of smoldering. To Zeke's left lay his father who was face down. To Zeke he appeared to be dead, but then the slight movement of his back showed that he was still breathing. Beyond Percy Proper, also lying on the hardened ground, but both on their sides, was Devon and Marjorie Anders. They too appeared to be either dead or unconscious, but then Devon moved his foot ever so slightly, his legs and arms still bound with rope. Looking passed Devon and Marjorie Anders, Zeke saw the Captain. He was still sitting with his back up against an old tree trunk, his arms and feet also bound with rope, but he was awake. Gnawing gingerly at the ropes around his wrists, the Captain looked like an overgrown rat chewing its way through a gunny sack full of food. The Captain stopped his chewing momentarily to look up at Zeke, almost as if he knew Zeke were watching him. He smiled, his grin awkward but sincere, his bruised face tightening with the effort, and then he waved at Zeke to come over to him.

Zeke managed to sit up the rest of the way without too much pain, although his head still floated as if he'd taken too much cough medicine. He got to his feet slowly. When he stood, Taylre looked up, her face lighting up like a bright torch; her smile spreading across her cheeks and radiating from her eyes with glee, celebration and relief. She rose up immediately and ran to Zeke, wrapping her arms around his shoulders and pulling him in closely. Zeke flinched slightly from Taylre's tight squeeze on his sore body, nevertheless he couldn't help but smile at the enthusiasm that Taylre put into everything she did.

Sniffing back more tears, Taylre said, "I...I thought you would never wake up. I th...thought you were dead."

Zeke pulled back from her embrace but still held on to her forearms. "I'm okay, Taylre. I'm a little sore, but it's getting better." He then turned to the Captain. "C'mon, let's get him untied."

They both scrambled over toward the Captain, aware of the others lying around them, but less concerned as they noticed Percy, Devon and Marjorie were beginning to stir, opening their eyes and starting to look around. When they reached the Captain, Zeke began to untie his wrists while Taylre worked on the ropes that held his feet.

"It was an amazin thing that ya did, lad. You are the bravest young man that I ever laid eyes on. Ya've taught me somethin here today," the Captain proclaimed.

Zeke looked up from his work. "Captain, I've got to be honest. I really don't remember anything that happened here last night. The last thing I do remember is standing back there in the weeds with Taylre, feeling like I was going to freeze to death."

Taylre stopped her work too, becoming flustered from the maze of knots that kept the Captain's feet together. "Are you trying to tell us that you don't remember *anything* that happened? The stones? The monster? The light? None of it?" she said incredulously.

Zeke shook his head, bobbing it a little and going back to his work on the ropes. The Captain and Taylre exchanged a knowing glance. Taylre grabbed Zeke's hands, stopping him from working on the knots and looked straight into his eyes. "Then have we got a story for you," she said, her face beaming with delight.

* * * * *

Percy Proper knelt beside the small campfire, its ashes still smoldering from the fire it held the night before. He blew gently on the glowing red embers that remained buried beneath a small pile of newly added kindling. A tiny flame erupted, grabbing hold of the dry pieces of wood placed on top and set them ablaze. More wood was added until the fire became, once again, a source of warmth and comfort.

The small group, including Marjorie Anders, Percy Proper, the Captain, Zeke, Devon and Taylre, gathered around the warmth of the flames. Noticeably absent were the three hooded men that the Mayor had hired: Walford, the Chief of police, Roberts, and of course the Mayor himself. Zeke looked around in confusion at the small group wondering where exactly the missing six men had gone.

Staring at him from across the fire, Percy Proper seemed to understand Zeke's thoughts. "They left," he said, rubbing his cold hands over the bright yellow flames.

"Who?" Zeke replied, his thoughts interrupted by his father's voice.

"The three men. Chief Walford. They left. I saw them go this morning, very early, before any light showed in the sky. They all looked sore, burned, and battered, just like the rest of us, but that didn't stop them. I've never seen four men more scared in all my life. Their faces were as pale as snow. I'm surprised they had enough guts to get in a boat on that river, but that's what they did. I'm pretty sure we'll never see any of those guys again. At least not around here."

Zeke continued to look around. "What about Roberts and the Mayor? Did they leave too?"

"You really don't remember anything do you, Zeke?" Devon said, speaking for the first time since he'd been laid out on the altar as the final sacrifice.

Zeke started to speak, but was interrupted by Marjorie Anders. "They were taken, Zeke, like all of us would have been if it weren't for you. You saved us all, and I thank you for that."

"But why can't I remember any of this?" Zeke asked imploringly.

"It's because of the stones. Their power was very great, but they couldn't have wielded that power if it weren't for you - your strength, your youth and your integrity. The stones used your inner strength to get rid of the Korrigan; to send it back to hell where it came from," Marjorie said.

"I don't understand," Zeke replied. "The stones were at the bottom of my box the whole time and I didn't know it. None of us did. Dad said they came from his dad, that he made them and put them in the box. So why did he have to die as a sacrifice? Why couldn't he have used the stones to kill the Korrigan?"

"First of all, you need to know that John didn't make the stones," Marjorie said. " He only made the box they were kept in. The next thing you need to know is that none of us, the Mayor, Roberts, me included, had any idea that the white stones actually existed. There were rumors and things written about them, but we managed to convince ourselves that they were just a myth. I guess thinking that made us feel bolder and somehow justified in what we were doing."

Marjorie Anders looked around at the small group seated beside the fire. She fumbled with her hands nervously, trying very hard to hold back the inevitable tears that so longed to flow. "I want to apologize to each of you, but I know that will seem a bit foolish and a bit late. And yet I beg for your forgiveness. I was misguided in my rebellious youth and I remain a misguided old woman." The tears that Marjorie had tried to hold back suddenly gushed forth, a sudden release of years of untold secrets and shameful acts.

Around the fire there was a feeling of awkwardness as Marjorie's friends and relatives watched her purge herself with her tears. Taylre then slid over closer to her grandmother and pulled her in tightly, hugging her and trying in vain to calm her shudders of pain and anguish.

As the light of day began to increase and the chill of the morning started to recede, Marjorie Anders stilled her crying. Embarrassed, she used the large sleeve of the robe she still wore to wipe away the tears from her face. With red eyes she looked up at the group who still sat by the warming flames. "I'm going to tell you everything that I know. After that, Percy, you can decide to do whatever you feel is right. I will submit to any punishment. I feel I deserve it."

Percy Proper shook his head and smiled weakly. "Why don't you just tell us your story first. Don't worry about punishment. Just know that we are your family...all of us," he said, indicating those who were seated around the fire. "And we love you, no matter what."

Marjorie breathed in a cleansing breath, preparing herself for her moment of confession. "Like I said," she began, "I was very rebellious when I was young. I got involved in a lot of things that I should have just stayed away from. David Vernon was a big influence on me, but just know that I'm not using him as an excuse. I made my own choices, and I'm responsible for them. Nevertheless, I should have tried to be more like my brother, John. He was always doing the right thing, and he warned me on more than one occasion to stop what I was doing. Anyway, one night, David and a small group of us were snooping around up here by the river when we came across this altar, at least what's left of it," she said, looking at the now crumbled and broken stones that once made up the stone table. "The altar was overgrown with roots and years of weeds and moss. So it was well hidden. It was pure luck that we found it...although, now that I think about it, maybe it wasn't luck after all.

"Inside the altar, buried underneath the rocks, we found a book. It had been well preserved and kept in a coating of leather and strong cords. We opened it and found that the first half of the book was written in a strange old language. The second half had been carefully translated into English and written on newer paper.

"We took the book home, always keeping it a secret, and read through it. It was there that we learned about the Korrigan and how we could become wealthy and prosperous for the rest of our lives. It's funny how none of us seemed to think twice about performing a human sacrifice; we were so caught up in wanting to be rich that none of us thought about any consequences. That was until we did the Selection Ceremony.

"When we found out John was to be our sacrifice, I didn't want to be a part of it any more. But they threatened me saying they would hurt me, or, worse, that they would hurt John's wife and children." She looked up at Percy, a deep sadness filling her expression. "I couldn't let anything happen to them. I didn't care so much for myself, but I couldn't stand the thought of any of them getting hurt over something that I had been involved in.

"Well, somehow John found out about what was going on. He confronted me and I warned him about what was going to happen; I told him that his family would be in danger if he didn't go along with it.

"Now, you need to understand that John was a very quiet man. You could never really tell what he was thinking, but I always viewed him as a fighter. Someone who would do battle to the end if he thought something was wrong or out of sorts. So when he said he would go along with the whole sacrifice thing, I was amazed. He was so calm and accepting. I suspected he was up to something.

"As things have unfolded here tonight, I think I've been able to piece together what John did." Then, Looking at the Captain said, "Bartholomew, jump in here any time if you think of anything that I might be missing." The Captain nodded approvingly, twirling his hand in front of him, urging her to continue.

"I suspect that John came out here and found the altar too. But his motivation was very different than mine and David's. He was looking for a way to stop all of this madness. I believe it was here, among the ruins of this old altar, that he discovered the white stones. I think he was intent on using them just like you did last night, Zeke. But he never got the chance. You see, David and Peter Roberts wanted to make sure that their chance at wealth didn't get the opportunity to run away, so they took him early, much earlier than John suspected. He'd hidden the stones for safe keeping. Keeping them hidden for the right time. But David and Peter got the jump on him."

The Captain grunted softly and the others turned their focus on him. "They took him from the boat, Marjorie. It explains a lot about the way he was acting during those few days before his disappearance. I only wish he'd confided in me. Maybe I could have helped to protect him."

"I'm not so sure about that, Bartholomew," Marjorie answered. "What you don't know is that they took Elaine, his wife. They used her as a way to get him to go along with the sacrifice."

"But I thought there had to be a willing sacrifice," Taylre said, still seated close to her grandmother and resting her head gently against her shoulder.

"Ah, yes. Well, a willing sacrifice where evil is concerned can mean different things. With dark magic and evil, a willing sacrifice is anyone who agrees, whether coerced or not," Marjorie answered.

Percy and the others nodded their heads in acknowledgement. They suddenly understood why Devon could take the place as the sacrifice. Even though he didn't really agree to being laid out on the altar, he consented because he felt his father would be in danger if he didn't.

Percy shifted uncomfortably. "You mean they threatened my mom? I had no idea."

"She tried hard to protect you, Percy. She, more than anyone, suffered the most. She feared for herself, and for you, and never said anything to anyone because of that fear," Marjorie said, sighing deeply at the memory of Elaine Proper and her quiet strength.

"When the ordeal with John was over," she continued, shuddering visibly at the memory. "The promised wealth and prosperity came. I don't know how, but it came. Things here in Alder Cove were better than ever in terms of money. The farmer's crops grew better, the fish were abundant and more and more tourists visited than ever before. The money just seemed to flow like a never ending river. But that didn't make any difference to me. I was sick and depressed all the time. I honestly don't know how I've managed to function all this time. Survival instinct, I guess.

"Then, payment for the loan came due, you might say. Thirty years of prosperity was all we were allowed before another sacrifice was expected. That's when they called you, Percy, offering you the job with the city, but really expecting you to bring your family. Because, you see, the 'sacrificial lamb' tends to run in the family."

"But I knew that," Percy said. "I knew what they really wanted and I was willing to do it simply because I thought my father chose to do it for the good of the community. But I didn't really know all of the details as it turns out, and I never suspected that it was Devon that they really wanted." He turned to look at Devon who was seated beside him. He pulled him in closely, hugging him tightly around the shoulders.

"I see now what a ridiculous mistake I would've made. I'm sorry," he said. "Please forgive me. I promise that I will try, from now on, to be the kind of father I know *my* dad would have been."

Zeke moved from the other side of the fire to be close to his father, sitting on his left, Devon on his right. They all held on to each other, relishing this moment of togetherness; feeling a true sense of family and love.

* * * * *

The Captain loosened the ropes that held his small boat secure. He climbed in carefully, his legs and arms still stiff from his earlier captivity. Balancing his way back to the stern, he sat down heavily on the wooden seat and let out a sigh of pain. Hours of sitting in one position while being tied up had taken its toll. The Captain grabbed hold of the pull rope that extended from the small Evinrude outboard motor and took a deep breath. Bartholomew knew that he didn't have much energy left in him to pull on the rope too many times. He closed his eyes and said a silent prayer, perhaps Odin would see fit to guide them all the way home. He tightened his grip and pulled as hard as he could. The engine sputtered and coughed, spewing out a torrent of blue-black smoke, and then roared to life. The Captain smiled and looked skyward, placing his hand to his forehead and making a little salute toward heaven.

Zeke, Devon and Taylre gathered together the belongings they'd brought along. Zeke looked over the ground eagerly trying to find the white stones, but then realized that like their inward power, they too had been used up and destroyed along with every other remnant of the pitiful curse that had plagued this area for so long.

They put out the small fire with some water from the river and then smothered it completely with handfuls of dirt. The trio then walked side-by-side to the river's edge where Percy Proper and Marjorie Anders stood waiting to climb aboard the Captain's boat. With the nose of the boat pointed downstream toward the mouth, the small group looked forward to reaching the marina where the waiting car would take them to their home and a well needed rest.

As the trio reached the boat, Zeke turned back to look once more at the ruined altar and the place where a small miracle had taken place. Then, very gently, as a slight warm breeze started to blow, a light rain began to fall, and the grass along the river's edge began to turn from a lifeless brown to a life-filled green.

Join Zeke in his next adventure,
Zeke Proper and the Serpent's ship

CHAPTER ONE

"Not Again"

Devon was dreaming again.

A heavy fog settled on the deserted main street of Alder Cove. The pavement was wet. Devon peered around in all directions, tasting the damp, salt air that clung to his moistened lips. He looked down at his hands, bringing them up in front of his face. Using the back of his right hand he wiped away the accumulated wetness that dripped from his forehead. All at once the thought that struck him was that the dream was not in fact a dream, but a very real experience. He could actually feel his hand dragging across his face. The pavement below his feet felt hard and substantial. The air was thick about his face, and as he exhaled, he could see and feel the puffs of breath that hung in the gray air before him.

He stood at the north end of Main Street where the road takes a gentle rise toward the foot of Odin's Pass. To his right, Devon could barely make out the sidewalk; the fog's mist settled on the ground, giving the landscape an eerie, ghostly quality. Devon felt a shiver run down his spine, the flesh of his exposed arms raised in tiny goose bumps. He turned to face down the length of Main Street, noting that he stood directly in the middle, his feet slipping slightly on the white line dividing the right side of the street from the left. A traffic light in front of him blinked yellow, a reminder that Devon should remain cautious. He began walking slowly, though the downward slope of the hill pushed him forward at a pace that became a little too quick for him. Dark shapes that were main street businesses, passed by as he walked. The buildings, however, remained shadowed and nondescript as the thickness of the fog saturated everything about him. Ignoring the buildings, for he felt no threat there, he trudged onward, hoping he was alone in this "dream" but he knew, somehow he knew, that there was another presence there. Someone, or something, that loathed him, that despised him beyond words or description.

Devon continued walking, wanting to wake up, but feeling compelled to push on, though fear rose from his bowels like a sickness that threatened to explode in a rush of vomit. He came, finally, to a familiar spot. The Captain's restaurant was located just a block ahead, and Zelda's Book Store was only a building or two past that. To his left was the gate that restricted non-boat owners from entering the private marina. But as he turned to look he noted that the gate stood open, its gaping entrance beckoning him to cross the threshold. Devon felt a momentary rush of surprise. The marina was private property. Entrance was permitted only to those who owned boats or operated a business on the sea-side, like the Captain's restaurant, or Zelda's Book Store. Devon recalled that only a few months ago he, Zeke and Taylre had entered the marina to search the Captain's boat for clues to the Korrigan. Entrance through the book store was the only option at the time. But now the gate remained open, and again, Devon felt compelled to enter, although his reluctance was substantial. He felt another shiver of fear run the length of his spine.

Passing through the gate, Devon began the steep walk down cement steps that eventually gave way to wooden docks where small boats rested. Here they bobbed gently with the easy rise and fall of the tide, their hulls slapping at the smooth surface of the green water. Walking further on, Devon made his way beyond the familiar docks and proceeded to a section of dock that was new to Devon, though the wood that floated on the green surface appeared rotted and withered with age. The sides of this pier were empty. As Devon peered down the length of the docks, the slated wooden surface faded into the distant fog, losing shape. He made his way carefully along the broken lumber, feeling the slick wet exterior on the bottoms of his bare feet. A slight movement to his right caught his attention, and the dock shifted as a small wave hit its side. Devon steadied himself, widening his stance and spreading his arms in order to remain balanced.

He looked up and suddenly a form appeared out of the fog, cutting through the mist like a dark specter. It loomed before him large and menacing.

The head of a serpent.

Its teeth were bared into an evil grin; its long neck covered in scales; its devilish eyes peering down at him, immoveable, without the slightest blink.

Devon reared back in terror, skidding on the slick surface of the dock and landing with a solid thump on his backside. Normally the pain of such a fall would cause him to wince and cry out, but his fear overshadowed any present discomfort. He began to frantically work his way backward, crawling crab-like on his hands and feet. He slipped once on the slimy surface of the dock and again found himself perched on his butt, his arms twisted painfully behind his back. Devon looked up again expecting to see the serpent-like creature readying itself to pounce and devour him like a frightened mouse before a hungry cat. But the monster remained steadfast, looking not at Devon, but toward some distant vista beyond the fog. Devon realized then that the monster was nothing more than a wooden serpent, an intricately carved ornament that decorated the prow of a large, ancient ship.

Devon exhaled a sigh of relief. He laughed nervously at his own foolishness and pushed himself up from his precarious position, standing once again upon the unsteady surface. He tried to brush away the damp and dirt that clung to his pajama bottoms, then stopped abruptly - pajamas? He realized for the first time that he was actually standing in the same clothes he went to bed with that night -am I sleepwalking? Is this real? He continued to gaze down at his clothing feeling a little silly and even a bit embarrassed. What if someone sees me? I'll be the laughing stock of the whole school. Then another feeling tugged at him, the feeling he'd had before of a presence. He knew it wasn't the serpent on the prow, but someone, or something real, an entity of flesh and bone, but something that hid in the darkness.

And darkness was its power.

Devon then looked up from his soiled clothing to once again peer down the length of the fog covered dock. From the mist there appeared a shape, a man, who slowly took form just beyond the serpent's head. He stood motionless, his head bent, his chin resting on his chest. Then, slowly, he raised his head and stared.

Devon gasped. The man appeared to have no eyes, just deep empty sockets where blackness swam, sucking light and energy into them. His facial features were shadowed and unidentifiable, though his hair appeared long, smooth and black, running down the length of his back. His shoulders were broad, and thick muscles pushed outward from the tight-fitting turtleneck sweater he wore. Then the man began to raise his muscled left arm from his side until he was pointing his finger at Devon. "Bring him to me," he said, although his mouth made no movement. Devon shuddered inwardly and fear grasped at him like a spring-loaded trap. He stepped backward and again slipped on the slimy surface. He felt himself falling and waited for the inevitable thump on the hard exterior of the dock, but the impact never came. Instead, Devon continued to fall, a never ending free fall into nothingness.

Behind his closed eyelids, Devon's eyes shifted rapidly back and forth, up and down. They stopped abruptly and slowly, ever so slowly, he opened his eyes and gazed at the ceiling of his bedroom. He gently pulled aside the blankets that covered him and sat up, swinging his feet over the edge of his bed and resting his feet on the cool, hard surface of the floor. He looked at his feet. They were dirty and wet. His pajama bottoms felt wet too, the hem of his pajama legs frayed and mud soaked. He ran his hands through tangled hair, ignoring the dirt that clung to them. "Not again," he exhaled deeply. "Not again," he said, shaking slightly as he tried to stand. "Not again."

LaVergne, TN USA
30 July 2010
191573LV00001B/1/P